MIRROR SHARDS

EXTENDING THE EDGES OF AUGMENTED REALITY

VOLUME ONE

PRODUCED BY THOMAS K. CARPENTER

Mirror Shards Volume One

Copyright © 2011 Thomas K. Carpenter
All Rights Reserved

Published by Black Moon Books
www.blackmoonbooks.com

El Mirador: © 2011 Alex J. Kane
Music of the Spheres: © 2011 Ken Liu
These Delicate Creatures: © 2011 Melissa Yuan-Innes
Below the Bollocks Line: © 2011 T D Edge
The Sun is Real: © 2011 George Page
A Book By Its Cover: © 2011 Colleen Anderson
Of Bone and Steel and Other Soft Materials: © 2011 Annie Bellet
Witness Protection: © 2011 Amy L. Herring
Stage Presence, Baby: © 2011 E.M. Schadegg
Gift Horses: © 2011 K.E. Abel
The Cageless Zoo: © 2011 Thomas K. Carpenter
More Real Than Flesh: © 2011 Grayson Bray Morris
The Watcher: © 2011 George Walker

Cover design by © 2011 Greg Jensen

Cover Images by
© Zach Dischner | Flickr.com
© Chris (UK) | Flickr.com
© Maria Keays | Flickr.com

ISBN-13: 978-1466205611
ISBN-10: 146620561X

This anthology contains works of fiction. Names, characters, places and incidents are ficticious. Any resemblance to actual events, places or persons is entirely coincidental.

CONTENTS

Introduction
by Thomas K. Carpenter

El Mirador   1
by Alex J. Kane

Music of the Spheres   17
by Ken Liu

These Delicate Creatures   39
by Melissa Yuan-Innes

Below the Bollocks Line   58
by T D Edge

The Sun is Real   72
by George Page

A Book By Its Cover   87
by Colleen Anderson

Of Bone and Steel and Other Soft Materials   100
by Annie Bellet

Witness Protection   122
by Louise Herring-Jones

Stage Presence, Baby   135
by E.M. Schadegg

Gift Horses   153
by K.E. Abel

The Cageless Zoo   176
by Thomas K. Carpenter

More Real Than Flesh   215
by Grayson Bray Morris

The Watcher   226
by George Walker

*To Trudy,
Enjoy the book!!*

MIRROR SHARDS
VOLUME ONE

Introduction

The term augmented reality, up until a few years ago, was one usually met with a blank stare, despite being in development for the last couple of decades. Only recently has the fledgling technology made enough progress to be noticed by the general public.

I first took notice in the summer of 2008 when I read a brief article about it in the *Economist*. The concept unleashed my creative mind to start devising ways the technology would irrevocably change society. I wasn't doing this as a futurist or an engineer, I merely wanted to write a series of novels and short stories around the concepts. Two of these novels, *The Digital Sea* and *Gamers*, are now out, with the follow up books in the trilogies due out this year and next.

After my initial exposure, I began writing a blog about augmented reality and eventually expanded to a second blog, Games Alfresco, when I was asked to join their team. I can say with great pride that I've helped chronicle the early adventures of augmented reality and in my own small way, helped shape its development.

But what I lamented was the dearth of fiction about the technology. While there are a smattering of books and stories that have hints of it, the only real novel to tackle the subject was the Hugo award winning *Rainbows End* by Vernor Vinge. A highly recommended read, I might add.

In this new age of publishing, power has moved away from the massive conglomerates too slow to adjust and too timid to take risks, to the writers themselves. With this in mind, I decided to produce and edit my own anthology with augmented reality as the theme.

A host of excellent writers responded to the call for submissions and in the end I ended up with thirteen fantastic stories showcasing the possibilities of augmented reality. Of special note is the story *Music of the Spheres* by Ken Liu. I designated it as the best story from the anthology (to me anyway) and gave it the Gold Award, which came with additional payments beyond the original offer sums. While I loved each story for a different reason, Ken's story exemplified the possibilities for the technology in our lives and besides being an excellently written story, it also fit the theme of the anthology best. Of course, I leave it to you to decide which stories are your favorites.

Lastly, you will notice a rather strange box on each of the "About the Author" pages. This is a QR Code, which is a primitive form of augmented reality. If you download a QR code reader on your smartphone or computer (assuming it has a camera,) the code will bring you to the author's webpage.

So if you enjoyed the author's story, feel free to take a ride through the QR code to their website and tell them. And suggest their story and the rest of the anthology to like-minded friends and family. If you liked it, I'm sure they will too.

Signed,

Thomas K. Carpenter
Editor
Black Moon Books

El Mirador

written by

Alex J. Kane

ABOUT THE AUTHOR

Alex J. Kane lives in the small college town of Monmouth, Illinois, a black hole from which he may one day escape. In the meantime, he holds a day job as a bank teller while pursuing a B.A. in English and writing speculative fiction. His stories have appeared in various journals and anthologies. Visit him online at www.alexjkane.com.

El Mirador

You wake to find yourself in a cramped, foul-smelling capsule spacious enough for one. After coughing up congealed phlegm and bronchial surfactant, you stretch your arms and legs, roll your neck, and glimpse the artificial world beyond the escape pod's porthole.

The Niven habitat El Mirador stretches out before you: a pearlescent band filled with verdant earth and vast oceans, its distant pinnacle arcing sunward to the point of near-invisibility.

A ping flashes in the corner of your eye; then highlights your destination, and marks it with real-time ETA and proximity data.

Two blinks, in rapid succession.

The pupil-centric indicator in your field of vision hovers to CONTINUE ON PRESENT ENTRY VECTOR, and winks green.

You rub the coarse sleep from your eyes, and wonder just how long it's been since you were put into cryo. Has it really been twelve years? Thirteen? Does the mission still stand, after all this wakeless time?

Pulling up the contract shows it was last synced with Astralum Corporation's database just over a month ago.

Valid. Incomplete.

You're still their dog, still on the hunt.

Just a highly intelligent, highly dangerous animal, as far as the suits on Earth and the inner colonies are concerned. The Lagrange points, they probably snicker from a coward's safe distance, befit an engineered killing machine like you.

All that wild emptiness.

The megastructure outside the pod draws nearer, but no red fireball licks at the pod. Not yet.

You catch sight of the flaring solar mirrors that regulate temperature and sunlight. The telescopes and lasercomm relays that speckle the vacuum all about the station like a swarm of winged insects, each pointing toward its own assigned in-system colony.

Memories come flooding back like the vague recurrence of some long-forgotten dream.

A name: Tzitzi.

Something about irony, flowers and a dead language on some plague-ravaged precolonial continent. Life prior to that of the mercenary huntress. Prior to purpose.

Untold debt, still waiting to be paid. *Ah,* you think. *That's what this bounty was all about. Yeah. Getting that shit paid off so I can buy my freedom. Clear my fugitive status, maybe even have fifty or sixty thousand credits leftover.*

Except that you know this one gig won't be enough. There will have to be more. You might go to sleep for months, or years, but debtorship doesn't ever freeze. It just expands.

You think, *Someday.*

Inside the ring's atmosphere, now — beneath the kilometers-high outer walls. A glow of rushing heat and fire. The rattle of air resistance.

Another name: Sol Mendoza. Your mark.

You pull the ripcord overhead; a practiced, reflexive action. This isn't the first time you've had to crash-land one of these half-assed excuses for a spacecraft.

Drag-fins snap out into the air behind the pod, reverse thrusters firing their explosive single-use rockets in a quick blast. The pod lurches sickeningly, and you stiffen in spite of yourself.

The ground below grows closer, closer...

Optical sensors overlay topographical data upon the visible terrain, and the craft's autopilot compensates for a level impact. To minimize damage; to the pod, to you.

A flash of forested green, and then the world falls dark.

§

Semiconscious and howling in agony, a good twenty-four hours or so pass. Meantime, a calculated spectrum of probiotics and autonomous nanobots in your bloodstream works diligently to seal the breaches in your dermis, nourish your hungry cells, and replenish the fractured regions of your reinforced skeleton.

Fueled by adrenaline, you manage to hurl the canopy open and gaze out at the world that encircles you. You reach for the edges of the ruined capsule, and pull at your own weight to heft yourself upright. Wincing, straining—

You're still far too weak to stand.

Try as you might to fight it, another blackout seizes you.

§

The nearby village settlement of Faribault sits low at the riverside. Concrete walls skirt along its borders, to keep the inhabited region from flooding. Scattered houses dot the rocky hills in the distance. Smoke and industrial filth curls skyward from the mess of belching factories on the edge of town opposite the river.

Wind turbines face upstream, their dizzying spiral dance supplementing the hydroelectric generators that jut from the floodgates. Churning, whining, tossing foamy spray.

This limitless data clouds your vision like so much eye-pollution, so much noise. Your cerebrospinal implant interfaces with the colonists' own network, and suddenly everything you'd ever care to know — more knowledge than any individual could possibly retain — is made accessible.

Is made *your own*.

No possessions, no citizenship on this world or any other, and yet even the impoverished exile can reap her fair share of the intellectual commonwealth.

"Okay, Sol," you whisper to yourself. *"Where are you hiding?"*

You strike out walking, headed for the settlement.

A tap of the touchpad tattooed along the inside of your wrist summons a list of recent queries. With an affirmative blink, the OmniWare device nestled in your brain stem seeks out any available intel on Mendoza's whereabouts via the town's surprisingly vast remote databank.

His identification sphere spawns in the air in front of you, immaterial but manipulable.

You spin it this way and that, perusing his personal history with a few flicks of your index finger.

This data is all public, but it beats the hell out of strolling into the pub and questioning the locals. This way, it's probably reliable.

Date and place of origin, last logged pass through customs, phenotypic profile, blood type, neural uplink make and serial number.

Last known location: UNAVAILABLE.

You pull the luminous sphere open, and examine the slivered facets of its interior.

All around you, folks are stepping outdoors from their rickety wooden homes to take a look at the outsider who's just wandered into town. Unbidden, untrustworthy. Fingering at the air like some insane mystic.

Offworlder, they silently sneer.

Save for some of the men, of course; some of them are craning their necks to ogle you with lusty eyes despite your alienness. Beneath your leather duster, the bulge of your breasts is still partially visible. Doubtless you're immensely welcome in Faribault, if these men have anything to say about it.

Striding on, pretending not to notice the curious eyes all about you, you head straight for the regional law office.

Inside the ID sphere, a single document catches your

attention. You scan it hastily, and simultaneously pull your hair back into a messy bun.

You think, *Now this is interesting.*

§

AstraCorp Headquarters. El Mirador Outpost.

The young man at the receptionist's desk is hunched forward, nose-deep in a tattered paper book. He doesn't notice you looming over him, not until you draw a breath and clear your throat.

My name is JARYN, his name tag reads.

You simply ignore the phantom cloud of information that hovers next to his head.

"Oh, sorry," Jaryn gasps. "Hello. How can we help you, Miss—?" The boy slaps the book closed, sets it aside, and taps at the glass panel on his desk.

A hologram flowers to life in the space between you, and his expression betrays supreme confusion when your face registers zero matches in the system.

"Tzitzi. Doesn't matter." You say, "I'm looking for a Solomon Mendoza. Goes by Sol. Heard of him?"

"Mendoza," the boy mutters. "Mendoza..." His dull eyes focus on nothing in particular as he seems to consider the name. Then he calls up a population master list, waves his way through thousands of names before pausing to ask, "He the guy who went missing?"

You sigh. Then, "What?"

"Yeah, hate to be the one to tell you, but if this is the same Mendoza, I heard something a few years back about an incident quite a ways upstream from here. Guy broke into a company storehouse and sabotaged a bunch of expensive farming machinery, maybe stole some too. Had help, I think, but he was the one in charge of the whole ordeal. Heard someone pissed him off, but clearly it was uncalled-for."

"And then...?"

"Then he supposedly just fell off the grid. Must've tossed his tablet in the river and took off. Something."

Speech analysis indicates he's telling the truth.

Meaning, of course, that Sol doesn't have a wetware implant installed any longer. He's all flesh. Which suits a barbarous outcast like him, you think to yourself.

In the pockets of your coat, your hands curl into tight fists. The boy, Jaryn, appears not to notice that you're shaking with fury.

The idea strikes you that this maybe isn't the best place to whip out a pair of submachine guns. Effective stimulus or not, they can't make Mendoza materialize right in front of you.

"Any *other* incidents involving him?" you ask, slowly leaning over the counter.

"I don't believe so."

Again, truthful. The kid's got no idea that on at least one in-system habitat, Mendoza is suspected — undoubtedly guilty — of murder; that the bastard routinely displays *alarming sociopathic tendencies,* as the AstraCorp network puts it.

With a flourish you stride back out into the warmth of El Mirador's reflected sunlight, en route to the wilderness that sprawls for kilometers upstream.

§

Waypoints mark concentrations of human presence in your path, which are few and far between. Trees like the mythic redwoods of old Earth tower all about, forming a canopy that drowns the soil underfoot in shadows. A cool wind follows you. There's the occasional cawing of a bird, but relatively little animal life to be spotted for hours at a time.

You come to realize that those winking green triangles off in the distance are your only beacon of hope.

They mark your progress, of which you'd have not even the vaguest sense otherwise.

They give you the drive to keep on, even as your stomach aches with hunger and your bones grow weary of the pseudo-gravity pulling you down.

§

Along the way, you access Mendoza's ID sphere for further study. Holovids of his last known public dealings, three-dimensional renderings of his face, and even full body scans. Local police logs of his habitual patterns.

The only reason you're on this backwater station is to track down Sol and spray him with a lethal dose of smoking bullets laced with paralyzing neurotoxins. And all the while, the smug bastard's walking right alongside you, a ghost of his past reality committed to digital memory just so he can taunt his pursuer.

Unkempt salt-and-pepper hair thinning to a high widow's peak. Cold green eyes, skin tanned dark by a working man's hours spent in the sun.

A wide, toothy grin as he swipes his credit chip, mouths

Thanks, asshole, and nods a solemn goodbye to the cashier at a general store somewhere in the territory. This one's a nonevent.

In another, this time a police surveillance record, Sol is leaning toward a young woman sitting beside him at a diner. They're finished eating, knocking back a couple of drinks, and he goes in fast for a kiss. His questing hand slips out of sight beneath the table. She backs away and wrinkles her nose at him in disgust.

He slaps her, hard.

She reaches up to touch her cheek with trembling fingertips, disbelieving. Tears glisten in her eyes as she slips out of the booth and flees, visibly mortified.

Doesn't take long before you decide this is all you need to know about the man whose life you're hoping to end, and wave the shattered AR sphere and its contents away.

§

Nightfall.

Nothing to hear but the wind in the trees, now. The river must be a day's trek away. The darkness carries with it an autumn chill. No solar mirrors visible up in the sky; only the faint light of the stars.

An indicator flashes, pointing toward something new it's just detected.

Following the blinking yellow marker, you come upon an abandoned camp site. A kindling burns in the center, putting off the lovely aroma of burning wood. Its embers have died down to a dim orange-red glow, but the heat it emits is a welcome surprise. You sit down on a large log beside the fire, and soak in the warmth.

Your implant brings up an optional chemical analysis of the burn, and you blink affirmatively.

The fire's only a couple hours old; at least since its flames were last fed firewood.

Curls of smoke waft heavenward from another fiery glow: the tip of a cigar at your feet.

You pick it up, sniff at it. Put it to your mouth and take a deep drag. The smoke burns your lungs and steals your breath. You cough, heave the tasteless puff back up, and hawk a wad of smoky mucus into the dirt.

You think, *Well, that's fucking gross.*

§

A quick search of the station's all-encompassing network confirms that the cigar is your mark's brand of choice. He's a tobacco smoker, all right. Before coming to El Mirador, he bought them by the crate, like the military does.

Traces of ammonia in the air form a trail leading toward Mendoza's safe house in your field of vision each time you force yourself to inhale the pungent byproduct of his cigar. You're just following his stench; chasing his filth through the woods while his own digital ghost leads the way.

"I'll take that AR with the scope, " Sol says to some faceless gun merchant. "Four boxes of ammunition, if you've got em."

Countless sales receipts: for sidearms, signal flares, an inflatable mattress, pieces of attire warm enough for living outdoors.

An order for credit line termination, per colonial law.

So you know he's well-armed.

Hell, any moment now a bullet might pierce your skull. Game over. But you've got a debt to pay, a life to buy back. Meantime, this lawless bastard Sol owes the authorities his freedom, at minimum; ideally his life.

Like so many, he isn't worthy of the air in his chest.

§

The next town you hit, where Mendoza's cigar smoke trail vanishes, is little more than a way station. A stop along the wheel that just keeps turning, pouring its infinite river on downstream.

Dawn breaks on the horizon, its golden light halved by the glittering band of El Mirador stretching skyward all around you.

A large unpainted vehicle trundles by on two sets of thundering treads, headed out of town. The sudden squawk of a bird on a rooftop overhead startles you, but you stifle your reaction and keep walking.

"Hello," says a little girl standing in the road. She grins, toothless, her ocean-blue irises gleaming in the sunlight.

"Hi there," you say. Then, "Do me a favor: Go inside and stay there, kiddo. Something bad's about to happen out here." You press a finger to your lips and make a shushing sound.

She does as instructed, and you let go a held breath. Relieved.

At the sound of her slamming the front door, you start back toward the center of the village, where several horses are tied in wooden stalls outside the general store and the handful of automobiles in sight all have the Astralum Corporation logo emblazoned on their sides in flaking, rust-scarred paint.

Then another sound, a metallic crack, stops you where you stand, and with a pivot of the heel you're facing back at the house where the young girl entered.

The long barrel of an assault rifle is aimed right at your face.

From behind its large infrared scope, a fat old man leans forward to get a good look at you. Gray hair, thinning to a high widow's peak. Dull, icy green eyes. Leathery dark skin.

Sol Mendoza.

Aged, but not enough to declare him nonthreatening.

A jagged scar runs down his cheek, starting at the corner of his left eyelid and disappearing into the shadow beneath his stubbly chin. His old eyes glint with a quiet intensity.

Fear.

"Sol," you say, only it's not a question.

The child appears again, clutching his pant leg from behind. He shakes her off, tells her to go back inside; she obeys.

"My little niece says you scared her, offworlder," Sol says.

And you say, "Did I? Just wanted to make sure she didn't see anything that might haunt her the rest of her life, like me killing you. Like seeing me throw your limp body into a burn pile."

"This old man?" He cackles.

You say, "Oh yes, Sol. Proper payment for your crimes is long past due. You want peace, you shouldn't go around murdering AstraCorp employees and destroying their equipment."

You say, "You've jeopardized this colony enough times. Now it's your turn to fall face-first in the dirt. Sorry." You offer a shrug of mock sympathy.

There's that grin: wide, toothy. A few teeth are missing, but the devilish lines in his cheeks and the crook in his brow haven't fled. Only deepened.

"Pardon me, stranger, but you seem to forget which one of us is staring at a rifle pointed right between her eyes." Another insane cackle, and he wipes a hand across his mouth.

"The people in this town appreciate you jabbing that thing at anybody who happens to walk by?"

He grunts. "Girl, the people in this town know to mind their own affairs, to keep their noses out. They know better than to cross *me*. You ought to take heed of their example, you want to get out of this place alive."

You smile, satisfied to be getting a rise out the old man. "I think you'll find I don't need your advice to survive. You always underestimate your enemies, Sol?"

"Not this time, I'd wager." Mendoza bares his yellowed teeth. "This time, I think I've found me just another loyal dog come all the way up here to die. For some damned corporation, don't give a damn about its own save for what they can exploit. Yeah, I'd say so. Another loyal dog."

You dive sidelong for the copper soil, reaching into the folds of your duster and pulling out the pair of Xing-Barron submachine guns you keep holstered below your underarms. After a momentous roll, you rise to your feet.

With a deliberate squeeze of the triggers, a spray of gunfire erupts from both muzzles.

The explosive cacophony of all those tiny sonic booms.

You keep your head low, strafing as you fire.

The light of a hundred flaring bullets as they burst free into the air, riddling Mendoza's ragged flesh and tossing up ribbons of blood in their wake.

He doesn't even get a chance to aim his rifle.

Instead, the life is flowing out of him like so much wasted potentiality, drowning the earth in an obscene pool of shining crimson as he slumps to his knees, and then collapses backward. He's heaving labored breaths, coughing up blood that streaks his face and drips to further soak the dirt.

You holster your weapons, and cross your arms.

Sol's young niece pushes the front door open, and a middle-aged man, probably Mendoza's much younger brother, steps out behind her. There are tears in the child's eyes as she hobbles down the stairs toward her uncle's motionless body. When the father on the porch gives no sign of confrontation, you give him a grave look, then turn and stride on.

In the nothingness before you, you summon the command interface of El Mirador's impressive lasercomm array with a few practiced strokes of your index finger. A rough 3-D rendering of the Niven habitat fills the space in front of you, and you prepare a voice recording to send out with the beacon.

The transmission will take months to reach the security contractors who sent you here, and a great deal longer than that before they arrive on-station to extract you. Until then, there will be plenty of time for exploring the luxuries of false liberty: whiskey, campfires in the wilderness, fishing for sport. Home-cooked meals, if you're lucky. Learning to smoke cigars the proper way, if you're feeling extraordinarily bold.

All this just to kill the time, and maybe even learn what it feels like to be human.

Before once more you wake to find yourself in a cramped, foul-smelling capsule spacious enough for one. Falling toward a new world; seeking out a new target.

Before you're unleashed to hunt again.

Music of the Spheres

written by

Ken Liu

ABOUT THE AUTHOR
Ken is a programmer, lawyer and occasional restorer of antique typewriters. His fiction has appeared in F&SF, Clarkesworld, Lightspeed *and* Strange Horizons, *among other places. He lives with his family near Boston, Massachusetts.*

Music of the Spheres

One time, when my little sister Lucy was almost four, she found a saran-wrapped half of a lemon in the fridge.

"Oh, I've never seen a yellow orange before!" She grabbed it and got ready to bite into it.

As the big brother, I was supposed to teach her about the dangers of the world. I explained to her that the "yellow orange" was not for eating. "You're really going to regret that."

But Lucy was skeptical. I had to show her how I had arrived at my conclusion.

I pulled off my glasses and put them on her, even though Dad had warned me that Lucy was too young to stare at augmented display screens.

I laughed. The glasses hung precariously on Lucy's tiny ears and button nose. She looked cartoonishly adorable.

Her pupils dilated as they focused on the ghostly layer of text and video now floating over everything she saw. I had set it to show content from *The Children's Encyclopedia*, and I knew what she would see as she turned to look at the lemon: the semi-transparent, looping video of a young woman making a face as she licked a slice of lemon, and scrolling text: *5% of lemon juice is citric acid*. "That's almost five times the acid content of orange juice," I said, showing off my command of mathematics. "So that means it's extremely sour."

Lucy took off the glasses and promptly bit into the lemon, and the expression on her face was priceless. (Of course I was the one who got in trouble later with my parents.)

For Lucy, reason would always come second to experience.

§

I was just the other way around. I became a math major.

I skipped a few grades and went to college early. Nervous about being younger than my classmates, I lived at home as a freshman instead of on campus. In the afternoons, Lucy and I would sit together at the kitchen table. She did her homework while I worked on my problem sets.

"Help me, Joe." She looked at me across the table one afternoon. "You're my only hope."

She was working on her first real proof, the one hated by every beginning geometry student: Euclid's *pons asinorum*, which required the student to show that the two base angles of an isosceles triangle are equal.

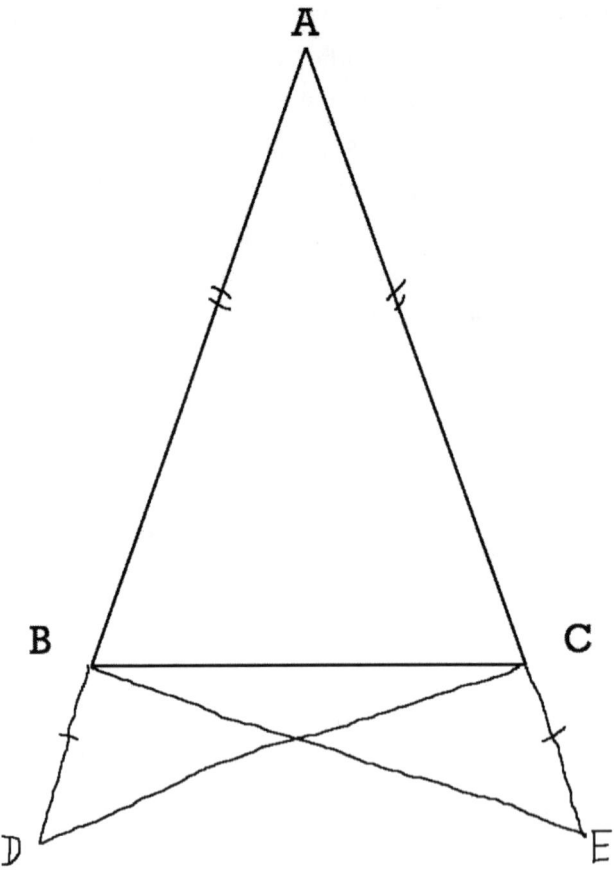

I asked for her glasses so I could see what hints and approaches her teacher had suggested. I stared down at the diagram on the workbook page and saw the ghostly overlay of helper lines added by her teacher to extend the sides of the triangle, BD being equal in length to CE. This was the classic approach taken by Euclid, and the lines created the set of congruent triangles that she could use in her proof.

I handed the glasses back to her and began to explain how she should think about the problem in a methodical, rigorous manner. But Lucy soon grew impatient. To her, Euclid was a meticulous fool.

"Just flip it over," Lucy interrupted me.

"What?"

"Just flip the triangle over."

She traced the outlines of the triangle with her pencil, pushing hard into the paper. Then she tore out the page of the workbook, flipped it over, and matched the mirrored diagram against the trace the pencil had pressed into the page below.

"The angle that was on the left matches the trace left by the angle that was on the right. So obviously they're equal. That's your proof."

For a minute I didn't know what to say. Her idea was in fact a version of the much more elegant proof that Pappus of Alexandria had come up with some six hundred years after Euclid. By imagining that the two-dimensional triangle could be "picked up" and "flipped" through a third dimension, it anticipated modern symmetry and transformations, but would have been considered cheating by Euclid.

"Aha," Lucy said, "I knew it. There was no need to bother with silly congruent triangles."

I recovered. "You can't do that. The Greek mathematicians thought about what you said, and they decided that your way was no good."

"Why not?"

"Your argument all depends on moving figures around. But 'flipping' and 'motion' aren't sufficiently well-defined given your current level of knowledge. You can't use them as proof techniques."

"But that's stupid. See, I just did it."

"Yes, but the fact that you can do something with models in life isn't helpful because math isn't *about* the models. It's not about anything in the world at all. Math is interested in logical structures that exist only in the mind. Anyway, the right way to do what you want is to use matrices and linear transformations, which give you a rigorous way to 'move' from one state to another. Stick to the congruent triangles for now unless you want me to teach you about coordinate geometry."

She maintained a sullen silence while I talked her through the steps of the proof, marking the triangles, identifying the shared sides and angles, citing the right axioms and theorems to use in each step.

I loved that blissful tranquility when you could see it all, each step of the proof supporting the next until the whole thing fit together like a row of dominoes, a logical push on the first inexorably, beautifully leading to the reassuring, concluding fall of the last. It was the Platonic music of the spheres. It was why I loved math.

Lucy wasn't impressed. "My proof shows *why* the angles are equal. Your way is so convoluted that by the time I get to the third page and write down Q.E.D., I don't even remember what I was supposed to prove."

"You just need practice. After a while you'll be able to hold it all in your head, and it will all seem intuitive. Forget about moving figures around for now."

Lucy grudgingly returned to the drawing. "*Eppur si muove*," she muttered under her breath.

§

During my last year in college, our parents offered to get me and Lucy augmented ocular implants for Christmas. The devices were new and quite expensive.

"Here—" The doctor pointed to a space behind the orbital cavity on a model of the skull. "—is where we'll put the implants. I suggest you get the modular seating, which is more expensive but makes future upgrades easier."

"How do I change the batteries in them?" That was my poor attempt at a joke.

"You don't. The seating contains a small dynamo hooked up to your arteries to generate power from the pumping flow of your blood. There is also a tiny fiber optic cable going from the implant through the optic disc into your eye—" Lucy and I both winced at this. "—don't worry, it won't impact your vision since that's where your blind spot is. The fiber optic cable allows the implant to project images onto the lens of your eye. That's how you get the informational overlay on top of your visual field."

"Why would I want this instead of getting non-invasive augmented display contacts?" Lucy asked.

"Contact lens displays are 'dumb' and can only show you information based on what your eyes focus on, not what's in your mind." I could see that the doctor was impatient with our uninformed questions. "But your brain is in a constant dialogue with your eyes, and most visual information comes *from* the visual cortex, not *into* it. The ocular implants are connected to your visual cortex so that they can tap into that eye-brain feedback loop. They'll let you *see* what you once could only *imagine*. It's a completely different experience."

I nodded, not really understanding.

"I'll need to run some tests on you first," the doctor said. "I'll call you next week with the results. Stop by reception on your way out to make appointments to come back for the surgery after New Year's."

§

"Hello. Is this Joe?"

The doctor's voice was soothing, compassionate, the voice of someone with bad news. I was out doing some last minute Christmas shopping. Crowds surged around me. I plugged my other ear and strained to hear the tiny voice through the phone.

About one person out of ten was incapable of supporting an augmented ocular implant. In such cases, the body relentlessly attacked the machine-brain interface, leading to blindness and worse. The problem wasn't well understood but the medical consensus was that it was probably genetic. Some brains, it seemed, were incapable of supporting a hardware upgrade.

I was disappointed but hardly inconsolable. An augmented ocular implant seemed like nothing more than a fancier version of the augmented reality glasses I was already used to. They were trendy and perhaps useful, but hardly essential.

"Thank you," I said, and hung up.

§

Lucy shared my genetic incapacity to have an augmented ocular implant. While I shrugged off the news, she took the issue more seriously and researched what our disability meant.

"Take a look at this," she said, and showed me a video she had found on the web.

It was a demo showing people how to make use of their augmented implants more effectively. The speaker, a research chemist, explained that the implant helped him do his job.

"When I read a paper about a new algorithm for protein folding, I picture in my mind how it would work. The implant takes these pictures in my brain and projects them onto my eyes so I can really see them."

The screen split in half to show the feed from his implant. A translucent model of a long molecular chain hovered in his visual field, folding and coiling itself into a complex knot.

"As I see the image projected onto my eyes, I can instantly change it just by thinking about it. Being able to really *see* the algorithm in my mind makes it much easier to work with it. It's like I have a way to immediately make a model and manipulate it with my mind alone."

The feed from his eyes changed to show two, four, eight, sixteen long chains folding and rotating in space, all in different ways.

"Even better, the implant allows me to maintain multiple visual models all working in parallel at the same time. Before the implants, the most I could do was keeping a couple of mental alternatives active in my head at one time. But now, it's like I had new RAM put into my brain, and I can keep track of many more alternatives all going full speed in my head at the same time. I literally feel like I'm ten times smarter."

The excitement on his face was palpable. He probably was exaggerating the effect a bit, but I thought I understood what he meant. When I first got my augmented reality glasses, I marveled at what I could do. Just by setting the right mode on the glasses, I could get definitions for words, encyclopedia entries for things, and instant results for complex arithmetic problems. I suddenly felt smarter.

But after a while, I realized that the feeling was only an illusion. Having instantaneous access to information didn't really make me smarter. The glasses were just a tool, like a really good and fast calculator. I still had to do the work to understand the concepts.

Lucy showed me more videos: designers who said that the visual feedback offered by the implant allowed them to create more effectively and with more originality; doctors who claimed that the implants allowed them to interactively filter through the latest research with their "gut feeling" and instinct derived from experience; children with autism spectrum disorders who explained that the implants allowed them to understand the emotional content of other people's facial expressions and body language and to connect them with their own emotional states.

"I think we're missing out," Lucy said.

I dismissed her concerns. The sense of increased mental capacity in these marketing videos was illusory, I told her. Augmented reality technology ultimately could not do the thinking for you, and it was thinking that truly mattered. My augmented reality glasses made it easier to study, to look up things, and to do the grunt work of arithmetic. And the augmented implants probably did a little more. But such tools were like slide rules and calculators, ultimately unimportant for a mathematician compared to the ability to move with ease among layers of abstractions and the pure insight needed for mathematical reasoning.

"We'll be fine," I said. I was reasoning from first principles, and my logic seemed unassailable.

§

"Lucy, can I come and stay with you for a while?"

I closed my eyes and held onto the phone, wishing for a lifeline. Around me, my studio apartment was a mess, full of unwashed dishes, empty pizza boxes, and torn drafts of my thesis, the thesis that I would never finish.

I had dropped all my classes for the spring. I hadn't left my apartment in a month. I wasn't even sure that I would go back next September to finish my Ph.D.

My old life, once so certain and simple, was over. And I could not bear the thought of facing my parents' disappointment. Lucy was my only hope.

"Sure." Her voice was calm and comforting. She asked for no details, demanded no explanations. She simply accepted my need. "Just email me your itinerary."

§

Lucy picked me up in Florida City, and we drove down Route 9336, the only highway through the Everglades. It was only April, but it was already too hot and humid for me, since my body had grown used to the many cold New England springs I experienced as a graduate student.

Lucy looked healthy and energized. She was settling comfortably into her new post as a junior biology research scientist. Sensing my need to keep to myself for a while longer, she took over the job of conversing for both of us. She told funny anecdotes about her colleagues and the joys and challenges of her work. I was grateful just to listen.

My little sister was all grown up, and now it was her role to protect me.

We stopped at the visitor center so I could pick up some postcards. During the short walk from the parking lot to the welcome center, mosquitoes and flies the size of my thumb buzzed around us. I was grateful for the bug spray Lucy offered.

She was always the practical one, the one who believed in solutions that worked. It was why I turned to her in my moment of crisis. Just being in her calming presence made me feel better.

The sea of sawgrass stretched around us in every direction, punctuated here and there with hammocks of gumbo limbo, oak, maple and hackberry, little islands only a few inches higher in elevation than the surrounding marl prairie. Ours was the only car visible on the road, and Lucy kept her foot on the gas pedal. In the passenger seat, I heard a constant stream of tiny pops as the giant flies and mosquitoes met their sudden deaths against our windshield.

I could see no animal life save the crows. In small groups of two or three strewn along the highway, they stood purposefully, as if waiting for something to happen. As our car passed, they turned and followed us with their eyes. In the rear view mirror, I watched as they slowly hopped onto the highway behind us.

"What are they doing?"

Lucy glanced at the crows and gave me a big smile. "You'll see."

We stopped at Pa-hay-okee Overlook, where we stood on the shore of a small lake, and twenty or so alligators sunned themselves contentedly, all floating within fifty yards of us. Further from the shore, a flock of roseate spoonbills floated gracefully on the water. At first I thought they were flamingos until Lucy explained that the wild flamingo population of the Everglades had gone extinct decades ago.

"The only flamingos we have left are plastic ones on people's lawns," she said. "The real ones didn't do well, probably because they never learned to adapt to people."

We admired the view until the bug spray wore off.

As we went back to the car, I saw three crows flapping off from the top of the hood to land nearby. From the bill of one of them dangled the wings of a moth. I looked closer and saw that the grille and windshield of Lucy's car were now picked clean of the dead insects that she had accumulated on her drive. The crows were treating Lucy's car like a sit-down buffet.

"A natural car wash," I said.

Lucy smiled. "Now do you understand what those crows back on the highway were doing?"

I thought about the crows waiting patiently by the road and hopping eagerly onto the highway as soon as we had passed.

"They were waiting for the dead bugs bouncing off the windshields of passing cars, weren't they?"

"You got it. Because cars go particularly fast in the park and the bugs are extra large, there's a lot of protein raining onto the asphalt all day long. So the crows in the park have learned to dine along Route 9336."

We drove on. Now that I knew the crows' purpose, my wonder only grew. But their relaxed attitude about getting their living from speeding tourists bothered me, somehow. I thought of the Everglades as a place of untouched, unsullied natural beauty, and the idea of crows living as parasites of automobiles seemed jarring.

"I study human-disturbed habitats," Lucy said, "which now includes every habitat on the planet. We're the most powerful evolutionary force the world has ever known. There's no pristine corner, no land untouched by Man. Even in the middle of the Pacific Ocean, there are floating islands made of our trash. Those crows are doing so much better than the flamingos because they adapted to our presence."

Suddenly my eyes felt funny and I had to turn my face away.

"What's wrong?" Lucy asked.

"I'm...thinking about the dead flamingos." I swallowed. "They were living their life just the way they always had, and suddenly the world changed around them without any warning, and they were gone. It's not fair."

Lucy put a steadying hand on my shoulder. "Joe, talk to me."

I composed myself. "Do you know the Four-Color Theorem?"

"It's the idea that any map can be drawn with only four colors, right?"

I nodded. The Four-Color Theorem was famous even among people who didn't know much about math because it was easy to explain and visualize. But for a long time, it was only a conjecture.

"It wasn't proven until 1976, when two mathematicians, Appel and Haken, finally presented a proof that seemed to work. But their proof was controversial."

Lucy snorted. "I bet it was controversial because they just said, 'Look! Give us a map, any map, and we'll color it! See?' And all the other mathematicians told them, 'No good. That's just reality.'"

I couldn't help but laugh along with her, remembering our days of doing homework together.

"You're pretty close. Their proof relied on an exhaustive enumeration of 1476 configurations that covered all possible maps and required a computer to perform the tedious details of the work."

"Well, was it *wrong*?"

"No, independent groups checked it and couldn't find any mistakes. But it *felt* wrong. Proofs were not supposed to require you to step through a laundry list of 1476 possibilities. Your brain could no longer see the pattern of the whole. And that was only the beginning. After that, proofs for other theorems also began to rely on computers checking through thousands and thousands of possibilities."

Lucy shrugged. "A lot of disciplines use computers for calculations. Nobody thinks that results are unreliable just because a computer did the grunt work."

I shook my head. This was so frustrating to explain. "Math isn't like the experimental sciences. We don't study things that have real existence. Proofs aren't based on 'evidence.' All we have is logic. You can't accept a result without understanding how it inexorably flows from foundational axioms. A theorem is important not just because it is true, but also for *why* it is true. The need to grasp the truth *intuitively* is why proofs need to have the right aesthetics."

"I never thought of math proofs as beautiful."

"Remember how you once thought it was more intuitive and convincing to do proofs by flipping figures around than by methodical deduction from congruent triangles? That's the idea: I couldn't feel that these computer-assisted proofs were convincing."

"But why are you the only one upset over it? Your entire profession must be having problems with these proofs."

"You don't have a problem with these proofs," I said, "if you have the hardware to understand them."

I finally told her what had happened.

§

That spring, I had been assigned to teach an undergraduate course on graph theory. One evening, as a little experiment and joke, I assigned my class the Appel and Haken proof with the expectation that no one would be able to follow it. My intention was to provoke some thoughtful discussion on the limits of mathematical intuition.

One of the students came to see me during office hours.

"I think I see a way to simplify the proof," he said.

"Oh?" I was amused. Every year a few students thought they saw a shortcut, and I had to disappoint them by pointing out the flaw in their reasoning.

He began his explanation. Thirty seconds into it, I knew I was in trouble. He knew what he was talking about. It had taken me days to get even a fuzzy picture of the kinds of configurations and their overall relation to each other. But he spoke of them as intimate landmarks, the way you would talk about the classification of books on your bookshelf. I resorted to nodding noncommittally whenever he paused in his explanation to look at me.

"Does this seem right? It feels too simple! I saw it the first time I read through the proof. Then the patterns came out more clearly when I went over it again. I could *see* it."

I nodded, hoping to placate him.

"You aren't following this, are you?" He stopped, and his face fell. I had given my seventh grade math teacher that exact same look when I enthusiastically explained to her my own derivation of Stoke's Theorem. She had nodded throughout my explanation, but I knew, at the end, that she hadn't *understood*. It was the first time I knew that I could see patterns that my teacher couldn't see.

Next to his temple was the silver glint of the access port for his augmented ocular implants.

§

"I was wrong," I said to Lucy. "These implants aren't like calculators, mere tools. They transform the human capacity for visual thinking. Students with augmented ocular implants can hold three hundred visualizations simultaneously in active contemplation as easily as I can hold two. They *are* smarter. They literally can see patterns that I can't."

For a while now my colleagues with augmented ocular implants had been publishing papers that I couldn't follow. I kept on making up excuses, telling myself that I wasn't interested in the topics or that I was just having a bad day when I was reading the papers. But I was living in denial. I had dragged out my time in grad school by years. It took the contempt of one of my students to wake me up.

Math was something I'd loved all my life, and I'd always been good at it. I'd worked so hard, sacrificing sleep and a social life. I dreamed of being famous, of making amazing discoveries.

And then, *wham*, someone invented a way to upgrade the brain of the human species, and some lousy gene in my body made it impossible for me to be upgraded, and I was supposed to just give it all up like that? I was furious at the unfairness of it all.

"You know, I've always envied you," Lucy said.

I looked at her, startled out of my self-pity.

"You were the one who had the genius IQ, the one who brought home the awards, the one that Mom and Dad always praised. Can you imagine what it was like living in your shadow? Knowing that I'd never be as smart, never as talented, never as *good*?"

"Lucy, I'm—"

"No, let me finish. I had to learn to find a place for myself in a house where your presence dominated everything. I couldn't read as fast as you, so I learned to be careful about which books I chose to read. I would never be as good as you at math, so I picked subjects where the requirement for quantitative reasoning was easier. I would never please my teachers like you did, so I had to learn to find praise in other ways.

"Living with you turned out to be good practice for when I found out that I couldn't get an implant. I loved biology, but I knew that I couldn't possibly compete in molecular bio against those who had augmented implants. So I picked ecology, a less sexy field where I could do what I loved without being at a disadvantage.

"Welcome to life, big brother." Lucy started the car. It was getting dark and we needed to get back to her cottage. "We all have to learn to live with change. Do you want to be a crow or a flamingo?"

§

I spent the rest of that summer following Lucy around the Everglades, as she taught me to see the wilderness around us in a new way.

I learned that the pesticides and herbicides used on the farms in Florida, Georgia, Alabama and the Carolinas all eventually made their way, by wind or by water, down to the Everglades, and all the species in the Everglades had to learn to live with them or die. I learned that the alligators and waterfowl populations in the park fluctuated with the industrial and recreational activities of park tourists and residents thousands of miles away. I learned that no square inch of our planet was free from human influence. All habitats were human-disturbed. It was just a matter of degree. The natural history of the last few thousand years has been one of the inexorable human effort to convert the biosphere to a human-centered symbiotic biota.

For Lucy this history was no source of despair. We were simply a force of nature, a part of that wilderness and the constant forces of change. Everyone could learn something from the practical crows.

Whenever Lucy tracked down yet another remote consequence of our activities on the planet, her eyes lit up and her face shone with happiness. It reminded me of the joy I used to experience whenever I worked through a particularly difficult proof and could see the beauty of the entire sequence, each logical step emanating from the one before, all of them together forming a harmonious whole.

I had once thought that harmony was something spiritual, something quite out of this world, like the music of the spheres. But just like Lucy showed me how the wilderness was defined, limited, changed, and given meaning by our work, I now understood that the sense of joy and harmony, that sense of rightness, of understanding, was defined, limited, changed, and given meaning by my biology. I could rejoice only in so far as I could understand, and I could understand only in so far as my body could adapt to the progress of technology. I was also a human-disturbed habitat.

§

I walked down the aisle between the two rows of desks, stopping occasionally to check on the work of one student or another. They were a bright bunch of twelve-year olds this year. I would like to encourage a few of them to think about taking Advanced Pre-Calculus next fall.

Laura, a studious and intense child, stopped me as I passed by her desk.

"I'm stuck."

I bent down to examine her notebook. In meticulous, dense handwriting, she had laid out each axiom, each derivation, each congruency pair. The lines of symbols followed one after another, cautiously, precisely, like a sequence of railroad ties going nowhere.

She deserved a break.

I took her diagram, and using her ruler as a guide, folded it down the middle of the isosceles triangle. I held the paper up to the light.

"Look," I said to her, "the two angles match."

"Yes," she said, uncertain.

"Q.E.D."

"Oh." Her eyes lit up. "I see."

She took the paper back from me. Now she knew which angles and which congruent triangles were important. I watched her fill in the last steps of the proof. Everything fit. Peace, and harmony.

A silver glint showed at her temple—they get them so young now.

Though I no longer dreamed of making amazing mathematical discoveries myself, I strove to show these children the beauty of math so that they could hear the music of the spheres as I did. Someday, perhaps one of them would make a discovery that I wouldn't understand, but would *know* is beautiful.

Laura and I admired her proof together. Then she turned her face up at me and we smiled at each other. Together we listened to the music of the spheres.

These Delicate Creatures

written by

Melissa Yuan-Innes

ABOUT THE AUTHOR
Melissa Yuan-Innes had to write a story for Kris Rusch, Dean Smith and Sheila Williams about a 90-year-old grandmother actress in space who was being blackmailed. "These Delicate Creatures" was the obvious result. Melissa is an emergency physician who lives outside of Montreal with her husband, son and baby girl.

These Delicate Creatures

Mem,

Stop acting.

Such a simple message projected onto the treadmill screen. It shouldn't have sucked the recycled air from my lungs or made me clutch the molded handlebar grips.

But I love acting. I love the smell of antique greasepaint smeared across my face. I love the heat of the audience's gaze. I love my parched mouth and the sweat pricking under my armpits as I extend myself into a new character. I love the one-eighth g on Cosmos 7 that allows me to bound and dance into the atmosphere, as if the air itself is another partner.

I love acting more than I have loved anything or anyone in my entire life.

I have received fan mail and hate mail in my time and become quite jaded about both.

But this message was a command.

This message used a pet name, a corruption of my real name, Emma Lo. This message penetrated my com link's filters in order to project on the nearest screen. The messenger cloaked him- or herself in anonymity: text instead of voice or video, and a blocked sender.

I sent a tracer on the message, even though I knew it was hopeless. I saved the script I'd been working on in the space condo gym. And I took a deep breath and grounded myself, just as if I had lost an acting part or blanked on a line.

I stepped off the grav treadmill, ignoring the hiss as it disinfected itself. My legs wobbled in a way I couldn't blame purely on readjustment to low grav. The air smelled faintly of sweat, even though the air purifier worked overtime as soon as someone keyed open the door. Although I was alone, I felt too exposed in a room anyone could unlock. I needed privacy.

I cut into our most opulent bathroom, centrally located between our gym and restaurant. It was soundproofed, illegal to spy on inside, and most thankfully, vacant.

The heavy plastic door sealed behind me. I stepped into the shower, fully clothed, and disabled the water module. But the next thing I knew, a woman panted in my face and writhed against my body while a man pumped her from behind.

I jumped out of the stall. A computer glitch had activated someone's shower porn. Murphy's law. I slammed the door, enabled the stall cleaning module, and called my director without further ado. "Quattra."

The first few bars of Beethoven's fifth symphony rang in my ears, louder than the robot brush scouring the stall behind me.

Then Quattra's image projected an armspan in front of me. She posed in a sheer white cloak that left her almost as bare as the shower porn woman. "Emma! I hardly recognized you."

I wished I could say the same. I suppressed a sneeze. Quattra was the only person vain enough to enable scent as part of her holo, even though the technology just wasn't there yet. She smelled like fake lemons and cloves, although maybe the former scent seeped out of the shower.

She continued, "The nanos have done a fabulous job on you. You look like a new man!" Quattra giggled at her own joke. At sixty-two, she was older than my daughter yet seemed even more juvenile. That was the problem with getting older. Everyone seemed newly hatched.

Except, perhaps, my wily messenger.

I bestowed a smile upon Quattra. "Yes, thank you. However—"

"The skin could be a little darker, though. And perhaps your voice just slightly lower, more of a baritone, although I like the acoustics in this space." She squinted at me. "I don't know if I should be honored or offended that you called me to such...intimate surroundings." She glanced down, realized her holo appeared perilously close to the urinal, and adjusted her projection closer to me, barely a hand span from my chest. She refocused on my face. "That's better. Remember, Emma, I would like your Othello to contrast even more with the rest of the cast."

Since Iago was played by an alien sea serpent and Desdemona was a human six-year-old genius, both nano-ed into

Caucasian adults, I thought she was bound by trivia, as usual. I reigned in my impatience. "Quattra. I have a serious concern."

"What's that, my darling? You need a pick for your new hair?" She laughed, shaking her own platinum tresses, and through the diaphanous cloak, I spotted her ears, nano-ed into clam shell shape. Lovely. She had already been listening-impaired.

"No. I am forwarding an anonymous letter to you." I blinked down a menu and eyed the send key.

She received it, scanned it, and laughed again. "Oh, Mem. What's the problem? An unhappy critic?"

I burned. Only my close friends and family called me Mem. Ever the actress, I swathed my emotions in sweetness. "In a manner of speaking. Do you think the President's entourage has any idea what we've planned?"

Her laugh tinkled once more. "Memmy. Darling. You think someone has leaked our little secret and the President of Cosmos 7 is threatening you personally?"

I allowed my mien, my silence, and our cloistered surroundings to answer.

She sobered. "Emma. You are, of course, the heart and soul of the production. However, if the President had an inkling, he would send in his storm troopers. Not a little message to you."

I shook my own close-cropped head. Quattra was the first to decry the President's maneuvers, from re-writing the Constitution to spying on and imprisoning "unpatriots" formerly known as citizens. That was why she'd spearheaded this play. But she'd never truly believed that the President would smite her, with the caveat that if he smote anyone, it would be the divine Quattra, not the eminent Emma Lo.

"Emma. Think of it this way. You have an understudy. The show would go on—crippled, maimed, irrevocably damaged without you. But the show would go on."

"I understand, Quattra." Subtlety was never one of her virtues. Whenever she felt besieged, she reminded us that we were replaceable. "But have a care, would you? I'll notify the rest of the cast in case they receive similar messages."

For the first time, two vertical lines appeared between her eyebrows. "Emma. You'd cause a riot! Wait until tonight's rehearsal, at least." Her tangerine, cat-shaped eyes compelled me, and I remembered that Quattra had been a renowned actress of her own generation, before she climbed on the director's chair.

"I understand your concern. I'll tell them at rehearsal." Prima Donna stereotypes aside, I could not have survived at my level of acting, for more than a century, without learning the tact and compromise worthy of a prince.

"Thank you, Othello." She blew me a kiss.

I severed the connection.

Almost immediately, a second message burned on my retinas. The anonymous mailer had hacked a direct com link.

Mem,

Stop acting NOW.

§

First, I pulled in a few favors. I direct-linked the most important person first. "Hertz? Can you trace an anonymous message for me? Stat?"

His avatar, a cartoon devil in a red suit, yawned. It took him a second to cover his gaping mouth, so I got a nice look at his tonsils and cleft chin. "What time is it?"

"I'm serious, Herskovitch."

At his full name, the devil stopped elaborately scratching his butt. "Fine. You owe me, Mem."

"I know."

"And one of these days, I'm going to collect."

He'd been threatening to do so for decades. Ordinarily, I'd smile and pat the devil between his tiny horns on his head. This time, it took all my aplomb to muster, "I know."

Next, I called my contacts at the President's office. Dangerous in itself. Could and would be traced. But as far as I could tell, our project had not yet been leaked.

So who had hacked me?

§

Desdemona showed up to rehearsal twenty minutes late and cranky. "She missed her nap," explained her mother. "But she's already better. The nanos are working hard."

I held my tongue. The nanos worked hard enough artificially maintaining Desdemona's decade-aged, sixteen-year-old body, without having to keep her hormones in line, too.

While Quattra's casting lacked a certain *je ne sais quoi,* she'd convinced the condo to add a micro-theatre for our troupe. We were able to squeeze in a stage, three rows of seating, two privacy screens to change and exit behind, a giant projection screen, cameras, lights, props, and best of all, the occasional live audience. It sounded grand, but it always smelled like popcorn and sometimes the floor stuck to your feet because everyone else used it as a secondary movie theatre.

While I eyed the blank projection screen, recalling the last Presidential speech about "justice" and "security," Desdemona missed her line. I could have prompted her, but I waited for the prompter on her com link.

Iago stuck his head out from behind the privacy screen to chuckle at her. It was more of a sibilant hiss. The nanos were still working on his vocal cords, although they'd managed to replicate the President's bland good looks.

Desdemona blinked her huge brown eyes. Uh oh. Cryfest time.

Instead, she whipped her juice bottle at his forehead.

The bottle smashed against the screen. Juice droplets sprayed against my face, hair and clothes.

Mm. Persimmon. I wiped it out of my eyes and my hand clung to my forehead.

Iago ducked, but fell on his behind and bounced skyward in one-eighth g. He screamed. He still wasn't used to navigating through air, let alone low grav.

"CUT!" Quattra screamed.

Iago launched off the ceiling, aiming for Desdemona's neck. I shot in between them, diving on the stage. "No!"

Iago bodychecked me. I rolled with it, dug my heel into the stage, rolled back to his side, and kicked him in the kidneys.

His eyes dilated. He wore the President's face, and the rage on it terrified me into immobility for one mindless second.

Ow! Desi yanked my hair from behind.

I twisted to bodybind her.

When Iago yanked her leg, ripping her away from me, I might have seized her ankle, except another message seared across my retinas.

MEM
Stopactingnow
Orelse

§

"Mem."

I squinted in the darkness. My temples pounded. My tongue felt like beef jerky. I tried to sleep a minimum of eight hours a night. At my age, you need as much beauty sleep as possible, nanos or no nanos. It took me a moment to remember the troupe's fight and the station police breaking it up.

A little red devil tried to crawl under the duvet with me.

"Hertz," I sighed. The plastic sleep pod, more of a cocoon, could barely accommodate my six-foot man form, let alone an unwelcome holo.

"I didn't want to wait," he said. "I found your hacker."

I pawed around my down blanket, my one item of retro luxury, for the ice pack hiding in its soft folds. The ice had reformulated into room-temp crystals, but I pushed it on my forehead anyway.

"Why don't you just get your nanos to lower the temp there? You're so old school," said Hertz.

"Look who's talking," I said. "You're older than I am."

He was silent for a minute. "Is all this worth it? This whole thing with the President?"

"He's a despot, Hertz." I slid the pack over my eyes. We'd had this argument before, his "let's just get along" vs. my "I can't get along with the space Gestapo." Or, as John Donne put it more eloquently, and I reminded Hertz, "'No man is an island, entire of itself. Every man is a piece of the continent, a part of the main. If a clod be washed away by the sea—'"

"Yeah, yeah. I'm the clod and the bell tolls for me." The devil caricature drooped his shoulders. "You really think this play is going to make him change?"

Every year of life seemed to pile up on my spine and yank down on my muscles. Still, I answered. "Most people don't take the arts seriously. They think they're 'a pageant/To keep us in false gaze.' But whenever a despot comes to power, he kills the artists and intellectuals. He knows we're dangerous." My mind, murky with sleep, surged on to the more pressing issue. "Is that who's threatening me? Were they interfering with Desdemona's com link too? That's why she screwed up her line."

The devil threw back his little horned blond head and laughed. "Nah. That was just funny. But I know who hacked your link."

Into the silence, I remembered one of Iago's lines: "I'll pour this pestilence into his ear." I waited.

He whispered the words. "It's your daughter."

I rocked backward. I couldn't breathe. I couldn't speak.

At that moment, a final message burst into my brain, complete with text and a booming male voice:

MEM

STOP ACTING

OR YOU WILL NEVER SEE

The message vanished. An infant holo projected above our feet. Sleeping. Legs bundled. Even on his skinny, newborn face and etched-closed eyes, I could trace my own original features. So real I swore I could press his heartbeat, pulsating through the soft point of his skull.

Someone startled him. His stick-like arms jerked to the side. His eyes opened. Dark brown eyes. My eyes. And a tiny but distinct cleft chin.

The infant holo vanished. My breasts ached even though I had never nursed.

I collapsed back in the folds of my duvet. Hertz's avatar leaned over me. His cleft chin quivered. He said, "We have to talk."

Instead, I called the one person who had blocked my link for decades. I threw open my sleep pod cover and she appeared, my grandbaby still clasped close to her chest.

"You thought I'd never have a baby," said my daughter.

Penelope's face was heavier than I remembered, more wrinkled, thicker around the jowls. Even her eyelids had begun to sag. She wore an unbecoming traditional navy floor-length smock and sensible shoes that might have been a school age uniform from the 1950s. No makeup. No nanos. Of course.

It startled me, how old my daughter had become. It meant I had truly aged, despite the miniature machines tending my every cell.

She had aged, but she was still arresting. My oversized nose and Hertz's cleft chin could have made her ugly, but she carried herself with such pride and defiance, she was something better than beautiful. Strong.

Yet tender. Even behind her American burqa, I could tell her breasts swelled with new milk. Unless she'd had hormonal injections, this was her birth son.

I spoke as gently as possible to her holo. "No. I thought you would have a baby. It was you who thought you'd never have one."

"Because of all your blanking nanotechnology!" If a holo could spit, she would have.

I felt Hertz's cartoon eyes on me. I murmured to both of them, "You don't know that's why."

"Yes, it is! You couldn't even have me until your fifties, with all the best doctors Hertz could buy."

I parried. "And here you are, in your fifties, with your own bundle of joy. Congratulations. What's his name?"

"Oh, no. You can't do this. You can't pretend everything's all right because after three decades—thirty *years*—of trying, we finally caved in to technology. You did this, Mem. I want you to make it right."

I tried to follow her logic. I remembered how everyone told me new mothers were irrational, hormone-ridden bags of tears. Until now, I'd always denied it. "I agree that I was one of the pioneers in nanotechnology."

"And in space! You kept going out to space, volunteering for missions. You wanted to be the first actor in space, Yahweh knows why—"

"I was a pioneer," I agreed.

"Our doctors are sure you did damage to your ovaries, with all the radiation and the nanotechnology. And you passed it down—you infected me!"

I remained silent. Science was not my strong point, but I once did a play about the DES scandal. In the 1970's, expectant mothers were given this medication against miscarriage, not realizing that their unborn daughters would develop abnormalities of their Fallopian tubes and a predisposition for clear cell cancer. I played a daughter who died from that cancer.

I bowed my head. "It's possible." I erased any doubt from my voice. It was Penelope's turn to take center stage, no matter how vehemently she would deny that. "But I'm very happy that you have a baby now. I know how much you wanted one." More than you wanted your mother.

She cried now, tears that snaked down her face. I saw one drip into the creases of her neck. She held the baby too tight—I still didn't know my grandson's name—and he protested. She turned her back to me. Her arms moved. I heard the swish as she unbound his swaddling. I heard his tiny lips smack. I even heard him swallow while she sat, back curved, arms cradled.

She was nursing.

I wanted to ask her to put her feet up. I wanted her to tuck frozen cabbage leaves against her cracked nipples. I wanted to hold my grandbaby so she could get, if not eight hours of sleep, at least eight minutes.

I wanted to mother her.

And I wanted to hold my grandson.

Instead, I waited and literally watched her back. Hertz's

avatar sat beside me and pretended to take my hand.

I let him. I knew better than most how much symbolism counted.

When she turned back to me, her tears had disappeared. The baby slept again. I risked a glance at his sweet, upturned face. His lower lip pushed back and forth a few times, sucking in his sleep.

"I promised Yahweh that if I got my healthy baby, I would welcome you back into my life. But look at you. You're an abomination. You're not my mother. You're not even a woman!"

I kept my lowered eyes on my grandson. His eyes blinked. His lips smacked again, but his lower lip pushed out rhythmically. He was dreaming.

"I talked to my pastor and my husband. We agreed that we will allow you to visit us on Earth if you forsake your... activities."

I met her eyes then. "My acting."

"Yes." She lifted her chin. At that moment, she reminded me of myself. The best and worst of me.

"You want me to stop acting," I said.

"Isn't it obvious? You love to reap the benefits, the body you can mold to your whims on the outside. But you can't help the corruption on the inside. You damaged me. You stole decades of children from me. I can't let you hurt our son that way."

Her words, so similar to the ones she cast at me twenty-five years ago, whipped old wounds. But the nameless grandbaby called me in a way I could not name.

I loved acting more than I loved anyone.

Until now.

§

"You left me, too," Hertz said as I curled back in bed, the down comforter wound around my knees, my eyes sightless at the plastic pod surrounding me.

I ignored his avatar.

"I knew we shouldn't have let her go."

Of course. And yet, when she reappeared, he called her my daughter. Not ours.

"'Whip me, ye devils,...roast me in sulphur,/Wash me in steep-down gulfs of liquid fire!'" I murmured to myself.

"Is that from Othello?" he asked.

And he wondered why I never married him. I blocked his avatar and dropped into dreamless sleep.

§

When I woke up, I called Penelope again. She was sleeping, but her eyes popped open immediately. She had prioritized my call above sleep. My heart squeezed in unworthiness.

"I can call back later," I said. Since she had disowned me, I couldn't locate her position on Earth, although I suspected she had stayed in the northern continental United States. She could be in any of three time zones.

She patted her son and pushed herself to a sitting position with hardly a grimace. Her bed appeared bigger than our theatre. The sheets looked like soft ultramarine cotton. A raft of pillows stood behind her. At least she and her husband had money and a baby. They had done well for themselves.

She said, "No, it's all right. I wanted to talk to you."

I smiled, but she did not. "You gave me up so you could act. But even with all your precious nanotechnology, for the past thirty years, you usually play old matriarchs. Crones. Aliens. Now you're even a black man. Was it worth it?"

I stayed silent. Somehow, she managed to knife me wherever I least expected it.

"My pastor says that in giving me up, you thought you'd be free to pursue your Art." Sarcasm made the capital A clear. "But instead, you crippled yourself, and your art, with your lack of humanity."

I wanted to kick that pastor in the testicles. If the pastor were a woman, I'd nano some testicles in before I walloped them.

But Penelope's wide brown eyes—like my own, like my grandson's—held me to the truth. "Yes. That's possible."

She sneered.

I swallowed. "Even probable. But has it occurred to you that I love you, I grieved for you, and—"

A strange smile spread across her face. The same smile she used as a toddler after she managed to unlock my trunk and smudge my antique collection of greasepaint all over her hair, clothes, walls, curtains, and bed. She cut in. "And you used that grief in your art. It was just another life experience you could use to grow as an actor. You use everything."

She was right. Even in the final shudders of orgasm, or

at the depths of humiliation—prostrating myself to Yahweh, praying for Penelope's forgiveness—a tiny voice inside me whispered, "Can I use this?"

That terrible smile widened across her face. Her eyes narrowed into slits. "I'm right. You know I'm right."

I can barely tolerate the young and smug. A middle-aged and petulant daughter calls for a good smack. I concentrated on deep breathing.

And my grandson. Penelope gathered him in her arms and he awoke without a cry, miracle of miracles. He lay against her breast, watching me. They say newborns can't focus more than a foot away, but I knew he could see enough from the way he surveyed me with open, intelligent curiosity.

I remembered the softness of Penelope's baby cheeks. Softer than rose petals, softer than the fur on our golden retriever's forehead. I remembered her questing, miniature fingers, her sweet breath, the determination of her gums as she bit my finger, yearning for milk.

"I love you," I said.

Her dark eyes burned into mine. "No. You love him. Jason. You never loved me."

Ah. Now I finally knew my grandson's name. Tenderness unfolded in my heart, made sharper by what was to come. "No. I always loved you. Every time I see a woman in traditional dress, every time I hear a little girl's voice..." My own voice failed me for a moment. "I think of you every night before I go to sleep."

She pulled Jason close to her chest, so close I could no

longer see his face. Her visible hand clenched in a fist. "What are you saying?"

"I love you. More than you know."

Her back jerked upright. "But."

"But the President must be stopped."

She rocked Jason, squeezing him to her chest. He yelled, muffled. She shushed him. She wouldn't look at me.

I spoke faster. "I love you. Thank you for sharing Jason with me. I love you both. If I'm still around after—"

She severed the connection.

Seconds later, Hertz messaged me. "I'm sorry."

I didn't answer. I knew he was leaving me, too. He had always yearned for a son.

I tucked the comforter, my one iota of warmth, around my shoulders, and I began to rehearse my lines.

§

That night, we hacked into billions of minds, beaming our story of lies and jealousy, the monster "[b]egot on itself, born on itself."

Iago preyed on our fears and deficiencies, working his brilliant, twisted machinations, while wearing the President's face.

Before my Othello died, I swore, "O curse of marriage,/That we can call these delicate creatures ours/And not their appetites!"

I recalled Penelope's face, the trust of her tiny body snuggled to my chest. I sent a breath of prayer to her and to Jason and yes, Hertz. I took another breath before my next line. "I had rather be a toad/And live upon the vapor of a dungeon/

Than keep a corner in the thing I love/For others' uses. Yet 'tis the plague of great ones/Prerogatived are they less than the base. /'Tis destiny unshunnable, like death."

Perhaps I had underestimated the President. Or perhaps Hertz's firewalls withstood his entourage's assault until that magical moment.

Only after the last word reverberated in my mouth did they sever our connections, smash our com links, and airlift us to our dungeons.

The ache in my chest, the hollowness in my lungs, the way I kept trying to blink down a menu or reboot my com link, my shackled wrists and ankles, the gag in my mouth...this was just the beginning.

But I summoned Jason's trusting face and I soared into my destiny unshunnable. My victory.

Below the Bollocks Line

written by

T D Edge

ABOUT THE AUTHOR
T D Edge has been a street theatre performer, props maker for the Welsh Opera, sign writer, adventure playground leader and professional palm-reader. He won a Cadbury's fiction competition at age 10; then, after the chocolate ran out, he got writing again to publish several YA novels and non-fiction books (writing as Terry Edge) with Random House, Scholastic, Corgi and others. A few years back, he attended the Odyssey Fantasy Writing Workshop where he learned a lot including, most importantly for an Englishman, how to hug. His short fiction has appeared in magazines such as Aeon, Realms of Fantasy, Beneath Ceaseless Skies *and* Flash Fiction Online. *He is also a freelance editor and writing coach; details at: www.thewritersark.co.uk.*

Below the Bollocks Line

A hum inside his head; an unusual hum of quietness that Bill Wilson tried to take for granted because he really did want it. Across the plain—plain and largely *empty*—wooden desk, a woman about his age all but glared at him.

"How did you get here?" she said; then, glancing at his file, "below the bollocks line, as you put it."

"Don't you know?"

"Do you want to stay?"

He glanced around the unplugged room, the hum already fading into pure, delicious silence. "Oh, yes," he said. "I'll die if I have to go back."

The woman wore a soothingly plain blue dress with her clear, pink arms folded in front of her—no logos, no animatattoos, no intelli-patches...

"Are you looking at my breasts?" she said.

"Sorry: I'm just so pleased to see them at all."

She might have smiled. "If you're to stay, you need to tell me how you got here."

§

"I can't see the damn teams!" Bill said to his son, Eric. "I've paid two hundred and fifty quid to watch this game and I can't even see the players. Are they really there?"

He squinted over the heads of the crowd, to the pitch which right then showed a giant electric car zooming up an empty mountain road. The white lines down the middle of the road shone brighter than the lines of the soccer field they covered.

"I told you to have laser-plus surgery, Dad. I said I'd pay for it."

"Why should I have to get my eyes upgraded just so the ads won't blare out the lads?"

He thought he saw dim signs of movement here and there, maybe the players warming up, but the car still dominated.

"I'll tell you who's on the ball," said Eric.

Bill looked at his son. Thirty-three years old, although you wouldn't know by his appearance: shaved head swirling in animatattoos—constantly changing scenes of muscular sailors, camp cowboys, winking drag queens. His face also changed every so often; now ebony skinned and holo-rendered like a West Indian, now white with an Eton-shaped nose. And his iSuit: nano-fibers rippling and expanding into a high-collared Sherlock Holmes tweed coat one minute, tight leather shorts and bondage shirt the next.

"I always meant to ask you, son," he said. "Do you mind that I'm not gay?"

Eric gave him a sweet smile, at least what Bill could see of it behind the philosopher's bushy beard now covering most of his chin. "It's not illegal to be straight, Dad."

Bill sighed. The pitch was now over-run by a pack of naked girls, rubbing age-reduction oil into each others' bodies.

"By God," he said, "does that really do nothing for you, Eric?"

He thought he saw the West Ham centre-back run out of a glistening blonde's shaved vagina, before disappearing between a glistening brunette's buttocks.

"I'm here for the footy, dad," said Eric, his tone slightly admonishing. "Besides, you know I've had the chop and tunnel op."

At this, Bill's apparently unfashionable todger deflated somewhat, despite the girls and the oil. But then the girls turned into a silver ant-eater sucking up piles of tiny black pound signs anyway.

"Don't you mind," he said, deciding to leave soon, even before the game began, "always being the one who gets screwed?"

Later, Bill's apartment door read his fingerprint and opened, the home computer singing, "Welcome, Mr. Wilson. I've selected some *heavenly* offers to suit your current needs—"

"I thought I told you to switch off all that crap, Sergio."

He walked into a miniature church-like scene of a dozen marble plinths, each bearing something that he apparently needed: a tofuburger and fries, a massage toilet seat, an animapuppy, and so on.

"This is the minimum exposure the government allows you for a rent reduction, Bill."

He also hadn't bothered to reprogram Sergio's voice, so it spoke with the government's default setting, like a slightly haughty but enthusiastic, probably gay Italian waiter.

"I'm not going to buy any of this bollocks, so can't you just bin it?"

"Only another thirty seconds, Bill, and don't close your eyes."

He threw his jacket on to the back of a chair then fell into the sofa, taking a childish delight in making his gaze go out of wack.

"I know what you're doing, Bill," said Sergio. "Please focus. I don't want the spooks to detect your non-compliance."

He did as he was told and the plinths soon enough vanished. Then the walls, ceiling and floor returned to their default settings—a mixture of mostly banking, holiday and health ads, all murmuring at the minimum permitted audio level.

"Screen," he said, and the wall opposite brought its ad for a personal genome scanner to an end, replacing it with a montage of six screens, the largest showing the afternoon news, the rest displaying random selections from the thousand-odd shopping channels he was connected to, like it or not.

He blinked twice at the main screen to call up the menu then selected the match he'd just left.

Three minutes later, the mobiloven pulled up alongside his sofa. He reached down for the tofuburger Sergio had already ordered, even before he had to watch the damn ad for it, and brought it up towards his mouth. His gaze remained focused on the game, now actually visible because the TV company had removed the ads from the pitch so its viewers could see the ads on the players' shirts.

"I'm only three percent fat," said the burger, "just in case you're watching your weight."

"Oh, for god's sake..." He took a larger than normal bite, hoping it would destroy the burger's voice mesh.

"You'll give yourself indigestion, eating so quickly," said the burger. "At least try to masticate more."

He held the burger at arm's length. "Is that meant to be funny?" he said. "Are you taking the piss out of the fact I live on my own?"

"No, sir," said the burger, "I'm just concerned about your health. Mastication is—"

"I *know* what mastication is. I just thought for a moment—silly me—that my wisearse food might have the personality to make a joke."

Before it could reply, he hurled it into the bio-waste bin, which quickly virtualed into a basketball net in the corner of the room, expanding briefly to catch the missile.

"Sergio, I'm going to spend the afternoon watching this game and getting drunk."

"Oh how delightful. I get to spend the day with a soccer retro-hooligan."

Which was the point Bill finally decided he'd had enough of all this bollocks and wanted out; to escape, to go somewhere no one would know about.

But he didn't say so right then. Sergio would only report it to a government mental health monitoring unit and they'd send someone round to cure him. Pump him full of nano-fixers which would seek out irrational and uncomfortable neural ether mesh matrixes, smooth them out, make him feel okay about his life again. Feel okay with all the bollocks.

No, he had to be cunning. So he drank whisky and shouted as usual at all the crap on TV. He went to bed and pretended to fall asleep, figuring that even if Sergio could tell the difference between real and fake sleep, he couldn't in any case actually read Bill's thoughts. Problem was, everywhere and everyone these days had cameras and microphones and spyfibers pointed at it. So, as soon as he outwardly expressed any desire to opt out, it would be recorded.

§

"It *is* recorded," said the woman in the blue dress. "Everything is."

"You remind me of Linda," said Bill.

"Your wife." It wasn't a question. "Who died just after giving birth to your son."

She really did look like Linda: stern forehead, strong jaw line, oddly kind eyes.

"What happened after you went to bed?" she said.

§

Bill disguised himself as a rug. At least, he kept as flat to the floor as he could, knowing Sergio's motion detectors didn't operate below thirteen inches. He slithered on his belly, feeling acid in his throat, cursing the whisky. He worked his knees and elbows across to the front door of his apartment. He stopped, facing the plassteel barricade that would open easily enough to his fingerprint, except the damn touch pad was four feet above his head and therefore in Sergio's range.

"Oh, sod it," he said, lurching up on his elbow and flinging his finger at the pad. "I'm half-pissed anyway. Who cares?"

The door opened as Sergio said, "Bill, you really shouldn't be going out at this time of night in your current state." Bill rolled through the opening, fingered the outside pad and laughed as Sergio pleaded behind the closing door: "I'm going to have to send an alert to the medical authori—"

Bill stood, took a deep breath, tried to walk confidently along the corridor toward the elevator. His blood field activated the corridor walls and they flared into images of commercial medications, mostly aspirin-based.

"Naff off! I'm not even hung-over yet."

§

"So, you were determined to get away from all the monitoring devices," said the woman. "You wanted to be alone with yourself."

Bill nodded. "Do you know, when I was a kid it was still possible to spend a few hours in a wood, just listening to the ants."

The woman frowned. "Our hearing isn't good enough to hear ants."

"I didn't say I could hear them. Me and a few mates used to build shelters under the trees and pretend we were in the Amazon, on the track of lost Inca treasure."

"Pursued by Nazi sympathizers and ruthless archaeologists?"

He smiled, too tired to wonder if she knew this from his file or because she'd been that kind of kid, too.

He looked around the room once more, enjoying the white, unanimated walls; the simple fiber lamps in the corners; her wonderfully plain blue dress.

"I pulled the hood of my coat over my face," he said, "and walked three miles to the cemetery. In the rain. With my head down in case the cameras caught a shot of my face."

"But you know they can—"

He waved away her words. "Yes, all the city's cameras are equipped with unique motor rhythm data matching software. Well, that was one reason for getting pissed first. I figured that and the anger would disguise my walk, at least for a bit."

§

The street outside flickered with lights from the flying cars above, the glass shields of the buildings either side absorbing it, leaving their panes free to summon advice and persuasion for the occasional pedestrian. Bill tried to close his ears to their whining endorsements and walked on, hating the softened surface beneath his bedroom slippers. Everything was safe today. Even an operation to turn you into a not-man.

In his unmodernised, unmedicated, booze-soaked body he felt both light-headed and full of internal pains. Real life, he reflected, should involve this constant and never complete balancing act between discomfort and pleasant befuddlement. Having one's gender inclinations, individual digestion matrix, emotional patterning and bowel regime constantly in tune with the e-verse around one, was just a recipe for bland.

"Hey, everyone," he said, "my son has a vagina."

He remembered cops, both when they patrolled the streets and later when they humped paperwork in their offices instead. He could do with a cop now, one he could smack in the teeth, who'd throw him in a cell where he could get a bit of peace and quiet. Except of course there weren't any prisons any more. Every cause of crime had been removed, just like his son's dick. Everyone had what they wanted.

He only wanted one thing. To sit in the earth at his wife's grave and get the soil under his nails; smell her spirit seeping out of the headstone. Feel, maybe, one last time, the welcome pain of the real absence of his spiritual heart.

§

"Had you forgotten?" she said.

"The whisky helped me pretend, at least for a while."

"The authorities switched off the cameras when you went inside the cemetery."

"Don't tell me they had a rare moment of humanity."

"I suppose they figured it was only virtual anyway."

"It all *looked* so real, at first: the cold, black shadows under the yew trees, the pale silver moonlight on the white heads of the marble angels, the tombstones all in different shades of dead. But the smells weren't quite right. I guess they can only simulate cellular decay. Can't fool your nose into sniffing the memory of her essence in the chlorophyll of the grass on her grave."

"But you desecrated her grave."

He shook his head. "Even the dead aren't real any more."

§

He found a spade in an unlocked hut by the edge of the cemetery. He plunged it into Linda's grave, hurling aside the sim-soil, determined to reveal the joke below. He dug for hours, sweat running down his arms and legs, the moonlight insignificant, and the bats and the pulsing coos of the owls.

He reached the wooden box, worked his way towards the hinged face-plate, uncovered it. He squatted, pulled at the upper lid, threw it out of the grave.

"My god."

A brief flash of muted bones, then Linda's face appeared, twenty-four years old, her small nose curved slightly towards the right.

Her eyes flickered open.

"Bill?"

Her voice, goddamit. *Her* slightly wavering top lip, the way it always did when she was unsure of something. Her shoulders rose as she tried to reach her arms out to him; he heard her knuckles thud against the lower lid.

"I want so much to believe," he said, then smashed the spade into her face: a brief flicker of blood splattering over his hands and then the face and bones and coffin disappeared; so too the earth and the owls and the cemetery itself.

§

"My name is Jane Harris, by the way," she said. "Doctor Harris. Believe it or not, we have no access to outside information here. All I have are the bare facts in this file, so I needed you to tell me how you really got here."

He relaxed a little, realizing her presence in this place was her choice too.

"Turns out that my lad—lass, whatever—Eric, has a good heart. I suppose I should have known that but it was kind of hard to tell, what with it being buried under all that virtual tat. He'd been worried for some time about his old man's mental state so he did a lot of nosing around on the net, under it, behind it and so on, to find this place. He'd made a deal with Sergio, too: to tip him off when I went over the top. Which was how he found me at the cemetery."

"And the file says he's paid your fee to stay here."

"Why *is* this place so expensive? I mean, your net bills must be zilch for a start."

"For the same reason it's so hard to find us on any comms system. We don't receive any advertising revenue. We pay for the food we can't grow ourselves without incentive discounts. Any decorating and maintenance has to be carried out with old, nano-free materials which are hard to find and costly. Even our laundry fees are much higher than normal."

"Because it comes back without images of naked chicks stroking your balls in return for you listening to them sweet-talk you into buying more crap?"

"Something like that. Walk to that window, tell me what you see."

Bill looked out on to green fields, darker green trees beyond, and behind them a line of grey-black mountains with patches of clear white snow at their tops.

He returned to his seat and smiled. "Nothing."

Doctor Harris nodded. "Nothing doesn't come cheap. Which is why we charge twenty years accommodation, up-front, non-refundable, even if you decide to leave early."

"Eric paid all that, for me?"

She handed him a handkerchief. He flinched after taking it, expecting that his snotty tears would just trigger an ad for online counseling or some such bollocks. But he took a huge honk into it and was delighted when all he saw when he opened it was greenish jelly-like snot.

"In here," said Doctor Harris, "it's safe to inspect one's excesses without the risk of attracting suggestions of commercial cures."

"I really do want to stay."

"All right, but why don't you sleep on it? We'll put you up in a guest room. Let me know your decision in the morning. It's a large investment by your son and I'm sure you want to make sure you'll honor it."

"He can visit me here, right?"

She smiled. "If he's able to survive for a few hours minus all that—bollocks—yes."

It took him a while to get to sleep. At first, he couldn't stop remembering Linda, especially now that nothing interrupted his thoughts: no talking walls, no singing street lamps outside, no gay waiter whistling while he bloody worked. But recalling her so clearly was painful, when all that existed in his mind was her and how he felt about her.

Later, he couldn't get to sleep because he was bored. He realized he'd be bored a lot here.

And that was a wonderful feeling to look forward to.

The Sun is Real

written by

George Page

ABOUT THE AUTHOR
Though many of his stories tend to be science fiction, George Page has written at least one short story in all the genres. His fiction can be found in anthologies such as Ruins Terra *and* Glitch in the Continuum, *as well as online at* Resident Aliens *and* Escapist Magazine. *He also wrote a novel of business:* Under the Gun: How to Start and Lose a Business in Six Months. *George writes in Fort Worth, Texas, sharing a house with three dogs who are worthless for editing or dictation. For relatively regular updates, his website is www.TGAPGeorge.com.*

The Sun is Real

A gentle hint of a heavenly perfume tickled his nose and pulled him from a dark dream of puddled blood, shattered bone and charred death. Without opening his eyes, he slid a hand forward to touch the silky smooth wall. This is real, he told himself.

"Please," a sultry, woman's voice whispered. "Won't you help me?"

He spread his fingers over the plastic mattress. This is real too.

"Only you can help me," the voice simpered with a hint of accusation.

Slowly, he rolled away from the wall to lay on his other side and, with a tired sigh, he opened his eyes. Trees surrounded him, and though he couldn't see the sun, dappled rays of light illuminated thick, soft grass. In the middle of this small clearing, just a few feet away, lay a woman propped up on her elbow. Or rather, in front of him, a goddess lounged.

"Just tell me where to go," she purred and leaned forward. Blonde, buxom, and gorgeous, she was wearing the familiar striated black and dark green fatigues of his regiment. Though with the pants slung low around her hips, the shirt tied-off to show a delicious midriff, and only one button holding back a sea of cleavage, she was definitely 'out of uniform.'

Another sigh escaped through his teeth; frustration, longing, and anger combined in a little hiss. That, he emphatically told himself, is not real. He rolled back towards the wall, invisible behind the projection of a vast, lush forest stretching out to forever.

She giggled. "Where is the rally point?" she asked in a breathy, 'come hither,' tone, and laughed some more.

Wishing he could close his ears as easily, he squeezed his eyes shut. The laughter didn't stop so much as fade over a distance. The perfume injected into his cell lingered long after.

He slept, for how long he had no way to tell. When he awoke, the forest and the temptress were gone, replaced by the default, featureless, pristine white walls of his five-by-five meter cell. He put his feet on the floor, and the plastic mattress squeaked a little against the floor. He scratched his beard and tugged on the end. He wished he knew in general how much time it took to grow a beard like his, perhaps then he could figure out the duration of his capture. It felt like enough time had passed for a beard to reach his knees.

It was five steps to the toilet in a corner, seven to the nook in the wall containing a paper cup of water and a ration bar, and four to his preferred sitting corner. The ration bar was devoured as he crossed the room. One of the earliest tricks they used was to randomly burst in to snatch his meager meal away. Sometimes they only sent in a projection of the jack-booted guard, but it always looked real enough to make him flinch. Today they let him eat in peace.

While he sipped his water, he called up the only book in his storage implant, placing it to hover without obstructing his view of the wall where the door appeared. By habit, he cursed himself for not downloading more books before leaving his ship that last time. But at least he had *Starship Troopers*, a quaint piece of science fiction taking place at a date over a hundred years before he was born. A story he had reread forty-three times within these walls.

This is real, he told himself. Not technically true, he could put his hand right through the floating pages, but it was the one thing they couldn't touch, or more importantly, use against him. He'd made the mistake of pulling up pictures of Elena during the first few days of his capture. And now... well, it was almost too much when they used her likeness against him, lounging seductively, tempting cruelly.

Everything else in his storage implant was encrypted milspec intelligence, and he dared not even think about the secrets behind the firewall. It was what they wanted. It was why he was still alive. And he could easily picture the bloody carnage and devastation that would result if the bastards got troop movements, locations and codekeys out of him.

To distract himself, he read his book. They could make him

see and hear things through his implants, but they couldn't touch what he brought out himself. In the beginning they had tried to torment him using a copy of his book with the words jumbled. Each time, though, he calmly projected his book on top of the copy and read on.

His reading today was interrupted when a door opened in the wall and Karl entered. Tall and imposing in a gray uniform and shiny combat boots, Karl had a hook nose, thin lips, and was bald—though it was unclear if it was from age or shaving.

"Hello, Bob," Karl said in his soft, dangerous way. "How are we today?"

Bob was not his name, but "Serial Number 428328" was the only information he had ever voluntarily given his captors, and even that wasn't correct. He had refused to give his name or rank as well, just to screw with them. In reprisal, they made up nicknames and flaunted fake-Elena at him.

Who am I kidding? They would have used her anyway.

"Look at what I have for you today," Karl oozed. As if with an invisible deck of cards, he made flicking motions, dealing out little screens that expanded and arranged themselves in rows in the air.

Zipping away his book, he looked at Karl's images. Looking was easier than the other things he'd tried; other things that bought beatings very much real.

Views of his regiment's soldiers and ships were displayed. Some pictures, the ones of carriers and dreadnoughts exploding in deep space, were taken from afar. The images of soldiers, however, were all close-up, highlighting the twisted and bloody remains. This is not real, he raged.

"Do you see?" Karl asked. "This could have been avoided. They fought because they had hope." Karl reached out, motioning to push an image forward. "Let's get to the heart of it: you can end this war, Bob. Give us coordinates. Give us codes. We'll overwhelm them, and they will surrender." A smile that never reached his eyes spread on Karl's face. "You can stop all this...dying."

Looking past Karl, he eyed the wide open door. As he had already discovered early on, it was no good. A painful twinge in his shoulder reminded him that more often than not, the door was not real.

"No?" Karl asked. "Nothing? That is disappointing."

Peals of delighted laughter floated through the doorway from a woman just out of view. It was supposed to be Elena's laugh, but they still hadn't gotten it quite right.

Karl turned to the doorway to call, "Coming dear," then glowered at his prisoner for a moment. "You know your usefulness has an expiration date," Karl spat. "We know the codes won't stay current for long. We know the missions will happen soon." Karl walked to the doorway, turning back as an afterthought. "What do you think will happen to you when the intel in your head is no longer relevant?"

A quick death, he prayed silently. Put me in a pod and fire me into a sun.

Long after the door sealed and vanished, he stared at the floor while Karl's pictures hung in the air, silently accusing him. He waited. Eventually they dissolved away, but so did the white walls. When he finally lifted his head, he was in a cage with thick bars and a low ceiling, dangling in a black limbo. There was nothing around, above, or below but palpable darkness. The cage made a convincing creak as he walked to his bunk and lay down. He stared past the incorporeal iron into the empty black for a long time.

This is not real, he told himself, and finally closed his eyes.

The cell was not plain and white when he awoke, but an ornate room resembling an Admiral's cabin on a carrier. Am I supposed to think these are Karl's quarters? he mused. Perhaps I'm to dwell on how my superiors are living while I'm stuck in here?

Seeing such thoughts leading down a treacherous path, he stood up on the plush carpet and walked to the toilet sitting awkwardly out of place in the fine room. Obviously, this shouldn't be real, he thought. Admirals have golden bowls in private Heads.

At the nook, he grabbed his meal then walked through a projection of a massive, oak desk to his corner, munching almost complacently. Just before he sat, he looked out the oval window behind the desk at the breathtaking view of a nearby planet with a glittering backdrop of stars. No sun though, he sighed.

When he turned away from the view, a magazine on the desk caught his eye. It was a puzzle magazine, and the cover promised 'hours of fun' with word and number games. He stood motionless, staring at it while finishing his ration bar and sipping his water.

This is not real, he assured himself, but with less conviction than normal.

He stood and stared at length before finally muttering, "Screw it." Tapping just above the cover and making a lifting motion, he raised the magazine into the air, then beckoned it to follow him to his corner. After getting settled, he brought the magazine down to eye level and motioned it open.

The first page was one of those ancient but still popular crossword puzzles. Flipping randomly, he found word jumbles, math puzzles, sudoku and hidden word hunts. It was a virtual smorgasbord of things to pass the time, if not rejuvenate his tired and stimulation-starved brain.

Glee sprung within, a surprising emotion after being so long absent. But its return reminded him of where he was, and how he got this gift to stave off boredom. So, instead of diving in, he merely pushed the magazine aside and watched the door-wall.

The door refused to appear, no one came to take the magazine away. Finally, he couldn't resist any longer and started on a puzzle.

At first even the easiest ones baffled him, his brain was like so much mush, and his fingers cramped writing letters in the air small enough to fit in the spaces. But soon enough he shook off the cobwebs and was gobbling up whole pages at a time.

This isn't real, he chortled in his head, but I'm sure enjoying it.

The crosswords were the most difficult as most of the hints were too obscure, so he felt a surge of accomplishment every time he got one right. He stuck to the most simple Sudoku and number puzzles, but even those were a great challenge.

The easiest for him were the word association games. He found absurd delight in the random things his mind came up with, especially when prompts like "badger" and "tough" made him write "Wolverines"—his platoon—and Sergeant Greene, respectively. Choosing Sergeant Greene was funny; the man was anything but tough.

A panel slid down to cover the nook for a few seconds, revealing his dinner when it slid back up. The movement caught his attention, but the timing surprised him. Had the entire day passed so quickly? He'd previously figured out that they sometimes altered his feeding schedule to upset his sense of time. So, naturally, he was suspicious, but a rumble in his stomach was proof that it had been many hours since breakfast.

A day has passed with no harassment, he realized half-way across the Admiral's cabin. That had never happened before, and it terrified him. Cautiously approaching the nook, he sniffed the water and ration bar. Everything seemed to be fine.

That means nothing is fine, he screamed in his head.

Torn between hunger and suspicion, he stood in front of the nook, hands pressed to his sides while lightly bouncing in agitation on the balls of his feet. He could picture them laughing in a room somewhere, watching his dismay, taking bets on what he would do, like he was some rat in a maze.

Will I take the cheese? he wondered. How can I not? came the dismal reply.

While picking up his meal, it occurred to him that if they wanted to poison or drug him, tampering with the food would be the most improbable method.

They control my oxygen. Hell, they sprayed perfume in here. They could easily squirt something else into my air anytime they please.

Oddly assured by the thought, he returned to his corner to eat and sip in bliss while working on another word-association puzzle. After only a few pages, he became sleepy and went to bed, further proof many hours had passed since breakfast. Before lying down, he raised up the mattress and positioned his puzzle book underneath.

The nightmares ran their usual course, and he opened his eyes with a lingering echo of fake-Elena's laughter. It had been vivid enough that he glanced around quickly to be sure. No, he was still alone in the Admiral's cabin.

With a sigh, he stood and went through his routine, but halted mid-bite on the way to his corner. Stupidly, he looked down at the great oak desk projection he was standing in, much like a huge, wooden hoop-skirt. It wasn't the desk that bothered him, it was that the desk and the Admiral's cabin were still there. They never left a projection in place for more than a day.

In a panic he threw himself into his corner while stuffing his face with the rest of breakfast. He couldn't decide whether to curl up in a ball, crouch, or crouch while curled in a ball. All the while, he kept his wide eyes glued to the door-wall, expecting the guard, Karl, or even fake-Elena to burst through at any moment.

The door didn't appear and no one entered.

What the hell is going on? Suddenly, he remembered the puzzles and skittered across the floor. Dismay was ready to flood him, but surprised delight took over when he saw the magazine where he had left it. The smile melted off his face as he motioned the magazine up to him.

Crap, he thought, are they killing me with kindness now, or just luring me into complacency?

Eventually he realized there wasn't anything he could do, so he plopped back into his corner to work through more puzzles.

It wasn't as joyous as the previous day though. Little doubts danced just out of mind, distracting him. The peaceful serenity of the Admiral's cabin was making him very anxious.

Determined to enjoy being left alone for once, he dove into the puzzles, starting with another word hunt. In the fourteenth row, a typo jumped out at him. It was an exclamation point, but there weren't supposed to be any punctuation in the puzzle. He had noticed two other exclamation point typos before in different puzzles, and each time he'd assumed it was an "i" upside down. This time, however, his eyes slid to the immediate right of the typo where "rescue" was hidden in the random letters.

Quickly, he flipped pages and searched until he found the first two typos. The words next to them read "hold" and "on."

It took all his self-control to not shout, hurl the magazine away, or jump to his feet. Instead he carefully scanned the entire magazine while desperately hoping his fingers weren't trembling too obviously.

There were only two more exclamation points. The full message read, "Hold on rescue fourth meal."

This isn't real, this isn't real, he chanted to himself, but only out of habit. Excitement, terror and tension rushed through him and he thought his chest might burst. Desperately he calmed himself, pulling the magazine close to hide his face.

Fourth meal? I found the magazine during breakfast, so is that two meals yesterday or one? Worry over the correct interpretation of the message was bulldozed out of mind by the sheer realization that his next meal here could be the last. And if not, then the one after for sure.

The urge to pace the room was overwhelming. Don't be an idiot, he raged at himself. Do what you always do: sit in that corner and wait it out. So he did, but it wasn't easy.

To pass the time, he dove back into the puzzles. His mind was racing, and he flew through the pages without stopping to think, scribbling the first answers that popped into his head. It was fun and carefree, everything he was going to be in a few short hours.

After an eternity, his stomach announced it was hungry. The rumbles were almost immediately converted to stomach pains, as tension clamped down. While he could breathe, barely, he could not tear his eyes from the nook.

Almost like in a dream, the panel in the wall slid down. A few seconds later it slid up. He blinked...hard.

The nook was empty.

His jaw slowly dropped, but before any other thought could register, he heard a muffled shout outside his cell. The Admiral's cabin shimmered and disappeared, revealing bare white walls.

He blinked again in the brighter light. There was a loud pounding, and the doorway appeared at the same time the door itself was kicked open. A man stepped into his cell wearing the black and dark green fatigues of his regiment.

"I'm Lieutenant Wilks. You ready to get out of here?"

In shock, he slowly rose and shuffled to the Lieutenant, though some part of his brain screamed to go faster. When he reached the Lieutenant's outstretched hand, he carefully patted it and rubbed the fatigues between his thumb and fingertips.

This is real, he told himself.

"This..." he croaked, "this is...real."

It must have sounded like a question because Lieutenant Wilks nodded with a twinkle in his eye. "It sure is. Now come on."

He was supported out of the cell and down a corridor until he felt able to keep up with the Lieutenant's trot. Along the way, Wilks spoke in low tones, bringing him up to speed.

"The Regiment never forgot about you. As soon as we learned you were taken, my platoon was dispatched to bring you back." Lieutenant Wilks paused at an intersection to make sure it was clear. "We caught up with the enemy flotilla a few months back, and have been tailing it ever since. This ship got detached for repairs a couple days ago, and we figured our best chance was a smash and grab before they got planet-side. So we hacked their mainframe and here we are. Did you get our message?"

He nodded dumbly at the Lieutenant as an explosion rang out somewhere down a corridor followed by the sounds of gunfire.

"I've got to get you to the small scout ship in the forward bay. The rest of the platoon is keeping them busy, and will retreat in our shuttle docked aft."

The Lieutenant hustled forward, made a few quick turns, then stopped in front of a hatch. He did something to the keypad and the hatch opened. "Get in and strap down!"

With a nod to the Lieutenant, he went through the airlock and sat in the co-pilot's chair. His fingers fumbled the harness into place, and he gave a thumbs up to Wilks strapping in behind the flight controls.

With glee, he looked out the view port to see a sun, and bathed his eyes in its magnificence. That sun, he reveled, is real.

The airlock closed and the artificial gravity shut off. Lieutenant Wilks grinned and started tapping displays, bringing the scout ship to life. "I'm sorry it took us so long to get you. They didn't hurt you too bad, did they?"

He gave the Lieutenant a shrug that floated him to the top of his harness. Almost shyly, he touched the dashboard. This is real, he exclaimed inside.

"Well, we're gonna get you back to the Wolverines in no time." Lieutenant Wilks tried to reach over to a display in front of the co-pilot's chair, but straps held him back. "Hey, do me a favor and input the coordinates for me?"

Nodding happily at the Lieutenant he reached out, but for some reason his hand just hovered over the keypad instead of typing. He squinted at Lieutenant Wilks, busy running up the engines.

The Lieutenant glanced up and smiled encouragingly. "Go on, we don't have much time. Sergeant Greene will want my ass for taking so long." Lieutenant Wilks turned back to his display, but continued talking. "Greene's a real tough sonofabitch, am I right? Thank goodness I'm an officer, or I'd be in real trouble."

Feeling like he'd been punched in the gut, he slumped in the copilot's chair, hand dropping lifelessly to his lap. *No, you aren't right, Lieutenant Wilks. Sergeant Greene isn't tough at all.*

Gingerly, the Lieutenant prodded him in the shoulder and asked, "Hey, you want to get out of here or not? Enter those coordinates and get us to the rally point."

He nodded and reached out. Again his hand only hovered above the display, but this time on purpose. For the first time since his capture he accessed his milspec data, quickly grabbing the appropriate system chart. With a little smile, he plot-solved a destination on the fly then checked the board. The engines were at full power and all system lights showed green.

Peace and relief replaced tension and dismay as he punched in the coordinates he had just calculated. As soon as he hit enter, his hand shot out to slam the jump-throttle to full.

No matter how hard they tried, he mused, *this was never real.*

The engines roared. Lieutenant Wilks frantically hit the emergency kill-switch to no avail: the ship was already squeezing through the warp-hole.

But that sun over there is real. And we're going to the heart of it.

A Book By Its Cover

written by

Colleen Anderson

ABOUT THE AUTHOR
Colleen Anderson's fiction and poetry have appeared in over 100 publications such as Black Quill winner Horror Library Vol. IV *(an honorable mention in Year's Best Horror) and* Evolve. *She is a nominee in poetry for this year's Aurora Awards (Canadian speculative fiction) and edits poetry and fiction for Chizine Publications. New work is coming out in* Polluto, Candle in the Attic Window, Witches & Pagans, Horror Anthology of Horror Anthologies *and* Bull Spec. *Colleen lives in Vancouver, BC. www.colleenanderson.wordpress.com.*

A Book By Its Cover

Syntia is ready to become her favorite show. She even has the bras and underwear like the Virtue Vis girls, Callista and Carlise; lacy, revealing not too much, firming and holding the breasts, making them mound up in amplitude even if she lies on her side or back. She had to try on over fifty bras to get one to fit and look the way it does in the shows. Eventually, she paid for implants, because when she lay down her breasts still sagged to the side.

She claps on the V.V. screen and sits, sipping a lychee-rice martini and eyeing her nails as the wall fills with color. *Soho Central:* who will she be tonight? Callista last week, even Bryce once; Luke has never been accessible. However, it looks like Luke will make the move on Carlise soon. Syntia grabs the programmer as the music fills the speakers and muffles her in sound.

She checks herself in the mirror that covers one wall before activating the ocular implants with three rapid blinks of her eyes. A seductive glance, she pouts, lips dusted with faint, shimmering mauve, then she slouches further into the form-fitting couch. Perfect. Not too much, not too subtle.

Her fingers tap the programming console as the images fill the dimensions around her. Now to play Carlise and get Luke where she wants him, where she wants to be.

V.V., Interactive TV. Syntia loves it. She loves being involved with the beautiful ones. They are all so glamorous and there is no reason she shouldn't have it as well. Callista and Carlise, models with smooth creamy skin, clothing that fits and moves perfectly on their sculpted bodies. Thin arms, firm thighs. Syntia has been practicing. She hungers to play these characters who entwine their lives in the fast times; the movers and shakers who built their empires on fashion and love and money. The men are gorgeous, tailored, successful, caring, with bodies the envy of any god. They *are* someone. Echoes of Syntia's mother saying, *"You'll never amount to much. You don't have the drive."*

Syntia wants more, always more. Soon, hopefully, the viewers will be playing Syntia on their Virtue Vis sets, programming her viewpoint into their consoles so that they will be her in *Soho Central*. She isn't sure how it works. An actor is integrated with the viewer but still acts true to the plot, which means there must be constructs, but Virtue Vis maintains that all their actors are flesh, and the viewer is just seeing what the actors see. And if they are real, then their fame can be hers. Syntia could lead a life as lovely and exhilarating as Carlise or Janeen, but for real.

Syntia sips her martini, and through the implants looks at her new surroundings. She sees Park Avenue as Carlise does while walking. Syntia has her stop and look in a few windows. The digital readout in one corner outlines the script. Viewers can direct the actors' minor actions, and view the show from a character's point of view, but the script is locked in. Carlise has a meeting with a fashion designer. No matter what one makes her do she will inevitably move toward that goal. Every once in a while Syntia tries some deviation.

Syntia-Carlise stops in an antique shop. The lean, craggy man walks over and smiles like an alligator. She smiles back and says, "I'd like to buy everything you have in the store."

The man smiles again and says, "Would you like to charge that? I can have everything sent to your place by this afternoon."

She walks out, snapping, "Never mind." The programs aren't always the most entertaining. It would have been nice to see shock or surprise on the guy's face. But still, most characters respond to her voice imprint and will follow a circuitous route. There are almost infinite numbers of minor characters for the viewer who deviates into little shops or such, but there's not much depth to them.

It had been expensive to buy the Virtue Vis entertainment system, so expensive that Syntia has foregone luxuries such as eating much. Besides, being slim helps her look like the actors, and it is well worth it. She's tried out for various shows. But that was before she started perfecting her image.

Syntia, as Carlise, bumps into Luke on the street. They share a taxi with opaquing windows. He confesses his undying love, his loyalty and search for the perfect woman. She coaxes him into parting the zip seals on her skintight pants and trailing his lips along her lean hip. It is still Carlise doing this, and no matter what Syntia sees from her point of view or says she still cannot experience the sensations. It would have taken millions for that type of set.

Luke and Carlise are still entangled when the taxi stops. Luke's business partner, who has been trying to bed him to gain investments in his new company, opens the taxi's door. Syntia as Carlise smoothes her pants, slides out of the car and smiles at the woman, then walks away. The episode ends.

Syntia sighs and deactivates the program, then checks her hair in the mirror. Still perfect, no strand out of place. She rises from the couch, one fluid movement, graceful, no jerks. As always, she is unsatisfied, hungering for the lifestyle she cannot yet afford, for being someone she cannot yet be.

Time to go out. None of her friends will go with her to The Club. Too trendy, they say. Snobs, they snort. Syntia knows better. It is just the envious sniping of those on the outside, the lesser class, jealous that they cannot attain that higher level and be integrated wholly with society's stars—those who really shape the world. She strips, then pulls on an emerald lycrex gown. It billows gracefully over one hip and cuts away to reveal her angular hipbone on the other side. It slips off the left shoulder in lightning jags and clings to her breasts like a lover. She turns before the mirror, arching her back just so. She smiles the Mona Lisa smile, the knowing smile that is just right: not too many teeth, not too goofy. Years have been spent perfecting herself and she knows others would love to see through her eyes.

She checks her makeup. Next to acting, it is what she does best. She likes to sculpt people's faces into masterpieces. Beautiful, living art from indistinguishable canvasses of flesh.

The cab is waiting when she arrives downstairs. Cars line up behind it. Syntia moves slowly, flowing, then stops to pull a smoke from her arm pouch. She bites the end. The other end flares red and she inhales before getting into the taxi. People stop to watch. She knows it, but will not look. Those who are truly the elite do not need to prove to themselves that others find them attractive. Even in the dark obscurity of the cab, Syntia remains poised. One never knows where a hidden cam might be.

The Club, the in-crowd is here. Atmosphere shoulders its way through the lights and music. There's no room for the uncultured smell of sweat. Syntia glides to a table, not too close to the front, not too central. Heads turn. Here she can watch the watchers without being evident. She leans back into her seat, one manicured hand slipping into the arm pouch, deftly removing another smoke. The end flares as she bites down, and smoke drifts lazily in the nearly clear air. Syntia prefers the smoky variety. They present an air of mystery, of sultry sensuality that envelops her. The smoke curls from her mouth, as if reluctant to leave her.

Slowly, she rearranges the folds of her gown over the covered hip. Who is here? Any talent scouts? Any agents or actors? The drink arrives in tinted glass, a mystery to those who wonder what she drinks.

"Hey, Cynthia, long time. You're looking good enough to

mold in holo."

Syntia glances up. "Markian, it's Syntia now. Ess Y En, no aitch." Markian is a round-faced young man, pleasing but moving nowhere fast. She wants far more.

"Whatever. You're still a deadly Syn to me." He straddles a chair. "Buy you a drink?"

She holds up her glass and smiles slowly. "I already have one. Thanks." She looks away and stares at the dance floor where those who dare to ruffle their exterior dance, avoiding a fatal fashion-marring sweat. She only dances when she can find the right spot on the floor, visible to those seated, giving a rare show, sure to look good from every side. After all, she has studied the shows to see how the stars dance, and has practiced before the mirror.

Syntia knows that image isn't everything but it serves to give you everything and get you where you want to be. And she intends to be there. Soon.

Syntia chats with Markian for a bit, remaining aloof. There could be other prospects, other possibilities to entertain. Markian moves off when Syntia declines to dance. She taps her holo-engraved nail against the glass, once, twice, but not so that she looks nervous—just bored.

It is time for a thorough look around, like Callista does in *Soho Central*. Take a sip of your drink, savor it; tilt your head to the left. Then slowly open your eyes; keep them heavy-lidded with sensuality, and roll your head until you're looking over your right shoulder. Not so much like you're inspecting the crowd as actually enjoying the visceral pleasures of the surroundings.

Visceral. Syntia could do with some heavy visceral pleasure. Her eyes catch on the man sitting to her right. He stares at her; she does not look away—doesn't show anything. She brings her drink to her mouth where her tongue laps the edge. He is stunning: chiseled chin, beautiful catlike eyes, nearly black hair in the latest style. His clothes look Armand and uncreased. The smoke from his cig forms a nimbus about his head. It is hard to tell in the flickering, swaying lights but he looks like Luke from *Soho Central*. Could it be?

Her heart knocks at her chest, reminding her of where she is. Don't look too long, Syntia tells herself. Not good to appear too eager. She lowers the glass, letting a half-smile touch her lips before she looks away and signals the waiter.

Syntia looks down and opens her pouch for another smoke, trying to formulate a plan to attract this particular man. He might have connections. A shadow blocks the lights reflecting off her lycrex gown. She looks up, unsurprised. It *is* Luke, and he holds a smoke out to her.

"Here, try mine." She takes it and bites the end. He doesn't ask, just sits beside her and orders a drink when the waiter brings her scotch.

"I'm Kieran King."

She clasps his hand firmly but doesn't shake it. "Yes, you play Luke on *Soho*. I'm Syntia Alleen."

They chat, warming to each other, gauging their moves. She gives him sultry stares. He gives her endearing smiles. She brushes his hand once. He leans in and lowers his voice.

"What do you do?" Kieran asks, leaning back and draining

his drink.

No point in beating around the bush. None of, 'I'm sure you hear this from every woman.' Just, "I'm in cosmetics, but I want to act."

More chat, then she asks him, "How long have you been an immersive actor?"

He smiles, a secret hidden behind his lips. "I do more than act. I only do that to keep a handle on what the industry needs. I'm the designer of Virtue Vision." He hands her a card with holo image.

She reads it, trying hard not to shake with the good luck she sees before her.

Virtue Vision
KIERAN KING
President
Our reality is yours.

Luke, the character, and Kieran King, good looking, rich, who will have pull in the right places. It is all paying off. She hands back his card.

"Keep it." He stares at her and says, "You are exquisite."

"Beauty isn't everything," she begins, the obligatory protest. "I'm like a book. The cover usually tells something of what is inside, and each page that you turn reveals a bit more story." It's one of her favorite lines. It shows depth.

"I'd like to explore this book," he grins. "Look, I might be able to help you audition for a part in *Soho*. We need someone like you. Janeen might be leaving us soon."

Curious, she asks, "Just how do you get an immersive program and an actor to mesh?"

"Come." He stands. "I'll show you the equipment."

Syntia takes her time. This seems so easy, too easy...but then she has worked hard to make herself into a Virtue Vision girl. It's no more than she deserves. She finishes her drink, feeling warm from the alcohol caressing her veins, then rises in one fluid motion, and exits beside Kieran, knowing everyone is watching.

§

They arrive at the Virtue Vis complex. There are filming studios and offices. The office is more of a high-story castle. To her surprise, Kieran does not take Syntia to the penthouse suite. They stop in the basement first. He holds the elevator door open, as polite as his character. Luke, the virtuous, the man who's made it to the top without harming others, the man who is loved by all—perfect.

He stops her in the lobby where there are plush green, form-fitting couches. He gives a short history of the operation, then puts a hand on her shoulder to guide her through another door. She turns to say something, and meets his mouth, crushing against hers, his tongue, sliding like wet velvet over her lips. His hand reaches behind her and pulls her buttocks towards him. His hips grind against hers. His mouth trails down her neck, biting softly.

Syntia gasps, giving her best performance. It is all an audition and men like to think they have the sexiest vixens in the world. But it is not all acting and fire spreads from between her legs. She touches one zip seal and releases it. He's already found the second, and her dress slithers to the floor like an abandoned skin.

Stockings and shoes are off in a minute. She's naked and releases the zip seal on his pants but he takes her before his clothes are dropped. He presses her down onto the couch, thrusting in—hot, sliding, moaning. Syntia doesn't mind the suddenness, relishes it. This is the ultimate power a woman can have over a man, to make him lose control. She arches her back, runs her nails under his shirt, moans deliciously into his ear; all he could ever hope for. Syntia is in control, loving the feeling but not giving in to it. Anything for an acting career.

But Kieran breaks through her control. He thrusts deeply and bites into her shoulder just below the neck. She yelps, thrown off balance as his teeth break flesh. Then he's pumping hard and Syntia gives herself to the moment.

A moment of rest, of acquiescence, before Kieran grunts and lifts his head. He smiles and kisses Syntia. She feels languid, limp, alcohol and sex making her like a sated cat.

"Let me show you where we make the programs," Kieran whispers into her ear. "We use a special implant." He picks her up, her weight nothing in his muscled arms. She wants to ask for her dress but feels too lazy, sleepy, and just lets him carry her. He walks past darkened doors explaining that Virtue Vis has top-of-the-line software, programs on the cutting edge. Full body integration for the viewer is just around the corner, and at an affordable cost.

She wants to look around but can't, realizing there is something off. She's never been this drunk. Syntia tries harder, to lift her head, to move, to say something and only a grunt escapes.

It is only when Kieran enters a low-lit room, one with many form-fit reclining chairs, that Syntia realizes her mistake. "We get only the best for *Soho Central*," he is saying, "and half a dozen other shows we run. Of course, virtual constructs are used in tandem with the interactive actors. The best actors are the ones that every viewer wants to be. Why are they so good as immersive actors, Syntia? Because it is their lives."

He's laid her down on one of the chairs. Out of the corner of her eye, she can see that some of the chairs are occupied. With all her concentration she manages, "K-Kieran, something wrong...can't move...numb."

He smiles an almost loving smile as he smoothes her hair from her eyes. "You don't think that was a love bite I gave you, do you?"

He takes certain small tools; wires, jacks, computer chips, from the counter in front of the chair. There are monitors lined up on them and some flicker replays of earlier Virtue Vis shows. He does something at her temple and at the base of her skull. He holds up an IV needle as if showing her a prize snake.

Her tongue is starting to work and she can turn her head but she can't lift her arm. "What...you doing?"

"You, Syntia, will be the newest actor on *Soho Central*. People will be able to access your personality and live through your eyes as you live as a projection in *Soho*. You'll meet all of them. I'm sure you'll all get along. After all, Soho will be your only life. You'll have some freedom to move in the scenarios but you'll never be far from me. I'm sure you'll be a great actress of the immersive world."

A pit is opening in Syntia's stomach. Panic wells blackly through her vision. "What do you mean? Why can't I move?"

"You're so perfect. It's what you wanted, isn't it? To be an actor, to live this world." He injects something into her arm and she cannot twitch so much as a muscle.

She always wanted to be an actor, live the lifestyle, but she never thought of the sacrifices. Syntia whimpers, trying to struggle but the neuro-toxin has paralyzed her. Her mind though, is fully active. Yes acting was her life but this isn't acting. This isn't life.

She gasps, "But you're not like this. You were so caring. Luke is so good and strong."

He stops and looks at her. "Didn't anyone tell you not to judge a book by its cover?" He flips a switch, punches some buttons. "You always have to look beneath the surface." He leans in close. "And that's where you'll be. Welcome to the stage of immersive acting."

"I don't want this. Please. Let me go."

Syntia feels her consciousness slipping into another dimension, but she struggles to hold on. "What are you going to do with me?" she whimpers. Already she can see and smell the streets of *Soho Central*.

"Oh don't worry," Kieran smiles and sits beside her on the reclining chair. He begins to undo his shirt as he strokes her breast. "I'll take good care of you."

Of Bone and Steel and Other Soft Materials

written by

Annie Bellet

ABOUT THE AUTHOR
Annie Bellet is a full-time speculative fiction writer. She holds a BA in English and a BA in Medieval Studies and thus can speak a smattering of useful languages such as Anglo-Saxon and Medieval Welsh. She has sold fiction to AlienSkin Magazine, Digital Science Fiction *and* Daily Science Fiction Magazine. *Her short work is available in multiple collections from major e-book retailers and her first fantasy novel,* A Heart in Sun & Shadow, *is available now as both an e-book and in trade paperback. Her interests besides writing include rock climbing, reading, horse-back riding, video games, comic books, table-top RPGs and many other nerdy pursuits. She lives in the Pacific Northwest with her husband and a very demanding Bengal cat.*

Of Bone and Steel and Other Soft Materials

Ryska froze as the staccato of Kalashnikov rifle fire rang out across the abandoned office complex. The length of copper wiring she'd tugged free of the crumbling wall hung in her hands as she focused on pushing away the memories that threatened to overwhelm her and tried to pinpoint where the noises were coming from.

The rifle fire rang out again, this time accompanied by angry male voices shouting. Not too close, probably coming from across the wide, overgrown square and beyond the low storage buildings near the main road. She relaxed a hairsbreadth and coiled the wire quickly before stuffing it into her bag. Her graphene whiskers twitched as Ryska cued them to a different sensory setting. She'd been running the sensors on low, letting her fingers and ears do the seeing for her while she dug the valuable wire out of the walls.

But with men around, she'd need more than her ears to get free of this place. Ryska mentally kicked herself for not paying more attention when she'd heard the truck noise. She'd figured they were just driving on by.

And where would they be going to? The glaciers? She shook her head. She hadn't seen anyone out here before and she'd gotten lazy. Lazy might have meant dead. Wasn't a mistake she'd repeat.

The landscape turned from foggy grey to many shades of blue as her sensors kicked in and the topography was revealed. Further away things were more blue than closer things, and objects with more solidity had more texture, fine lines zigging across them. Her sensors helpfully mapped out the clearest path out of the building with a hazy yellow line.

More rifle fire. Closer. Ryska pressed herself against the wall and rubbed her chilled hands together slowly. Not her problem. She'd get to her cycle and then *bamph* from this place.

Somewhere, close, a young boy screamed and the memories that Ryska had fought off earlier came slamming home. For a moment she almost called out to him, he sounded so much like Luka.

Ryska let out a shuddering breath. She wasn't in the lab outside Irkutsk. She was in the old city limits of Tynda. Safe. Free. Unlike Luka or Gregr or Misha or Iosif or... she slammed her fists into the wall, the vibrations emanated out in fine silvery lines as her whiskers picked them up but the physical pain dragged her away from that horrible night of fire and death.

Govna. More shouting, coming from the square, meant

that the men with Kalashnikovs were between her and her cycle. She flicked her head to the right, picking up the scrabble of movement just as a small body, outlined by her whisker sensors in shades of red, rolled through the doorway and curled against the wall.

"Hello?" a small, timid boy's voice whispered. "I need help. Is someone here?"

Ryska bit her lip. It was night, the building should have been too dark for him to see her. She studied the blue landscape around her, discerning windows in the wall facing the square. She didn't think they had glass anymore and some had been boarded over judging from the lack of air flow and the solid blue coloring. The men outside might have electric torches and flashes could be illuminating the room. That was not good. She had to get moving.

"Please?" the boy whispered again, crawling across the floor toward her. "Help me." He stank of fear sweat but his voice, his little red hand reaching out toward her, those things froze her.

Luka had reached the tunnel with her. If he hadn't insisted she go first, he would have been the one safely away instead of her. She hadn't been able to reach his hand. The damn tunnel had been his idea, he'd wanted to tunnel out of the lab so they could go find the bears rumored to live in the dead forest outside Irkutsk. He'd wanted to touch a bear.

They'd been so young. So stupid. Ryska shuddered but the decision had been made miles and years away. She slid toward the child and caught his hand, his fingers warm and slightly gritty in her own.

"Shhh," she murmured. "Follow me." The least she could do was get the kid away from the men with guns. Succeed now where she'd failed before.

Ryska led the boy down a hallway, following the hazy yellow line toward another doorway. She had to get to her cycle. Once on it, she could slip down one of the dilapidated pathways and head into the city, dropping the boy off somewhere with a telephone.

Cold air hit her exposed cheeks beneath her goggles and pressed her whiskers back against her face as they reached the opening. She sent a quick command to the control board implanted in her chest and brought the sensors up to full power. Her kinetic battery would run down after less than an hour of this, leaving her blind again, but she needed to know exactly where the men were and what they had. To get that level of detail, her sensors had to run at capacity.

Even so, the fog of war, as Gregr had jokingly termed it, enveloped the world beyond twenty meters. Within her sensing range, four figures moved across the square. She hardly needed her whiskers to "see" for her with all the noise they made. Their electric torches were outlined in white as they stomped across the square, slashing at the tall, dying grasses with their rifles as though trying to flush out game.

The boy's hand squeezed her own tightly, as though afraid she might let go. He must be the game. She didn't know why men with rifles would hunt a little boy, but his fear of them was thick enough to taste. She ducked back into the room as one of the blobs of white flicked her direction.

"If we hide, will they give up and go away?" she whispered to the boy.

Red lines flickered about his head as he shook it. "Those are the mean men who took me. I guess they killed Sergei and his guys. He was trying to rescue me." A sniffle followed this hushed disclosure.

Great, she'd ended up in the middle of a kidnapping, apparently. Or it had walked on top of her, in reality. The men hunting the boy must have felt comfortable leaving wherever the initial gunfight had happened, which meant they'd probably killed the rescue party just as the boy assumed.

Ryska searched the area beyond the door. There was another building, this one with multiple stories, just ahead. They'd have to dash across the open ground between, exposing themselves for a moment, but the yellow haze said it was the clearest way through and still somewhat in the direction of her cycle.

Crouched in the doorway, Ryska watched the red shapes move toward each other, grouping in the middle of square. Men's voices drifted to her, too low to make out. No white shone in her direction. Time to go.

She pulled on the boy's hand and darted out into the open, trying to move as quietly as she could. The boy followed on her heels, still holding her fingers in a death-grip.

Just before she crossed into the light blue of the doorway, Ryska tripped. Her foot slammed into a hard surface, catching on what was probably a cinderblock she'd missed in her dash. She swallowed the cry as she went down hard, barely catching herself with her left hand and skittering a foot across the gravel and weeds. The boy went down with her but she jerked him forward, half throwing him through the doorway even as she scrabbled to her knees.

Bullets bit into the wall as she rolled through the doorway.

"Go, go," she hissed to the boy.

"I can't see," he said.

Ryska stood and grabbed at his arm again, pulling him along the yellow line. If it was too dark in here for the boy to see, it would be dark enough to hide them.

"Go around, but don't shoot the boy, you *dolboebs*," a man's voice called out and she heard feet crunching on the gravel outside. The hunters were trying to flank.

One red blob appeared in the door just as Ryska and the boy ducked into another room. A shout meant he'd seen her.

Ryska took a deep breath. Her heart was racing, the control panel in her chest aching as it drew power for her sensors. It always felt like a wound just beneath the skin when she taxed it, but she needed the vision she no longer had. Vision the men hunting this boy wouldn't have if she took their torches away.

She shoved the boy toward dark blue of the far wall and pulled her pick-axe out of her belt. Pressing herself against the wall, Ryska waited just inside the door for the red blob to cross the room.

Predictably for a sighted person, the man came into the room with his torch and gun first. Ryska didn't bother trying to wrest the gun away from the big man. Instead she ducked low and swung her pick-axe into the white blob. Glass broke with an ozone-scented hiss and the man fell back, cursing and flailing wildly with his rifle.

Ryska dashed across the room and caught the boy's hand again, half-dragging him away through the building. She slammed back against a hallway wall as two more men came through a far door and sprayed bullets across the crumbling drywall.

The only direction that was clear within her sensor range was a stairway going up just across the hall.

"Stay low," Ryska whispered to the boy, shoving her pickaxe back into its loop. She didn't wait for his vibrating red nod but pulled him with her as she bolted like a crab across the hallway. White blobs and shouting almost overloaded her whiskers on the right side as she crossed the danger zone, but then the stairwell was in front of them.

The boy stumbled over the first step. "Stairs going up," Ryska whispered, reminded again that he was blind in here.

The cold metal railing felt good on her scraped hand but the air was clogged with drifting light blue dust disturbed by their feet. The dust worried her. They were leaving tracks for the men to follow.

The stairs opened up into another hallway. The floors in here were clear of debris, so the whole topography had a yellow haze over it. Safe and easy to move around meant it would be easy to follow them. Ryska shuffled her feet and didn't see the same drifting bits of blue that signified the thick dust on the stairs. That was something, at least.

Ryska pulled the boy along the hallway, running as quickly

as she dared. The clink of boots on the metal stairs made her increase her speed. This wasn't going to work. With the boy blind in the dark, she wouldn't be able to outrun the men and now they were trapped in a building she'd never been inside before. There might not be another way down.

She crossed into one room and then another, searching for a way back to the ground. The doors to the rooms were long gone, probably salvaged for timber and metal. The sounds of pursuit had faded beyond her hearing and she slowed, letting go of the boy as he stumbled again. His gasping breath would give them away if she didn't let him rest. *Govno*.

"What's your name?" the boy asked, sinking down into a red puddle against one of the dark blue outer walls as Ryska paced the room, testing the boarded up windows and trying to think of a way free.

"Ryska," she said softly. She heard a shout, but it sounded as though it came from further away. Good. The men were moving in the wrong direction, unless they'd split up. She froze, held her breath and listened.

The hushed rasp of the boy's breathing was all she heard. Ryska slipped out her pick-axe and tapped the lighter blue section, a plywood sheet nailed across a door-sized opening on what she thought was the outer wall of the building. She managed to slowly pry away the edge and felt along the outside. There were the remains of a balcony out there from what her sensors were able to tell her.

"I'm Toma," the boy said, though Ryska hadn't asked. "Toma Turzakov."

Ryska froze. Turzakov. It had to be a coincidence, but somehow she figured it wasn't. "The Railway Demon?" she asked softly, easing the plywood back into place.

"That's what some call my papa," Toma said with a tremulous hint of pride in his voice, the sound of a boy who'd been teased about his papa.

A smile played at Ryska's lips. Misha had used that same tone when they'd teased him about being the son of Trainer Kirakov.

The Railway Demon was not a man to tease, from what she'd picked up in her quick bartering forays into Tynda proper. He controlled a syndicate that ran the railways and kept a stranglehold on what little timber Tynda still had after the world had broken and turned its crown to ice. She berated herself for even thinking it, but rescuing this little boy could come with big rewards. No wonder these men wanted him.

She should leave the boy, the men wanted him alive, after all, so he wasn't in real danger. With the darkness to her advantage, she could get away. Toma would be ransomed, though hopefully better than whatever had happened outside that got those other men gunned down.

"Ryska?" Toma said softly, as though trying to determine if she were still there.

She bent over him and slid one hand into his hair and felt him sigh heavily with relief. His hair was tangled but soft and smelled warm and human, a little like bread left in the sun. Her fingers conjured the memory of another boy, another soft head of hair.

"It's blond. That means yellow, like butter." Luka laughing as her fingers tugged on his hair.

"I remember," she said, trying not to sound petulant. *She did remember some things from before the virus took her eyes. The domes of Kazansky Church, like fluffy blue and pink-red candy rising up against a grey sky. She even vaguely remembered the sky, a huge expanse of shifting colors above, blinking with stars in the darkness, deep and cold.*

"Now you'll remember me, too." Luka smelled like honey, probably from stealing packets from the Trainers lounge inside the Lab.

Remember. Her fingers curled tight and Toma gasped, pulling away from her hand. She couldn't forget. Not with their ghosts living in her heart like bright after-images of the stars she could no longer see.

"Ryska?" he said again, this time with a little fear in his voice.

The Lab was gone, their program shut down in a hail of bullets and screaming children. For a moment the skin behind her goggles burned as sealed tear ducts tried to bring tears to useless eyes that had long ago been removed. Her whiskers twitched and for a spare second the small red shape of the boy seemed to multiply and become two little boys huddled in front of her.

"I'm here," she said, unsure if she spoke to Toma or to Luka's memory. "Tell me, quietly and quickly, what happened to get you here."

A shuddering breath from Toma and then she felt him shift

and straighten, curling his knees into chest as he became an even denser red shape. She knelt beside him, her head turned toward the doorway so that she'd have maximum reception for her whiskers if the men came this way.

"I was at school and then when Dimah picked me up she was scared." Toma took another breath. "There was a strange man with a pock-marked face in the car and he wasn't Grigori, my usual guard. He made Dimah drive out of the city, to this warehouse and then..." Toma broke off in a gulping sob and Ryska could almost taste his tears as he struggled to go on.

"Dimah's dead." Ryska made it a statement, not a question.

She felt him nod as he continued, "They held me in this room, six of them I think. Then they said they were going to take me to my papa but they shoved me in this trunk and it was really cold and dirty and they drove forever. We got here I guess and then the men took me out of the trunk and I was happy because I saw that Sergei was here so I thought maybe he'd take me home but then the pock-marked man argued with him and then everyone was shooting so I ran and saw you." He pushed it out in a rush, his voice rising and then abruptly breaking off as he reached the end.

Ryska rose to her feet. It was about what she'd suspected. No help would be coming for this boy anytime soon. The ransom or whatever it was had gone wrong.

"Toma," she murmured. "I need you to trust me. I'm going to get you out of here and back to Tynda."

"Why? Because of who my papa is?"

The question and his slightly suspicious tone surprised her.

She revised her estimation of his age upward and felt something akin to respect for the boy. He'd followed her without question up until now, but was mature enough to recognize she had no stake in his survival.

She debated for a second and then told him the truth. "You remind me of...someone I loved."

"Like your brother or something?"

"Yes," she said with a sad smile, "exactly like that." And because of who his papa was and the reward she might get, but Ryska felt that the boy might take offense to that and she dearly needed his cooperation.

"Okay," he said.

She reached down and felt along his rustling parka to his hand. "Come with me," she said. She showed him by touch where the opening in the plywood was. "Crawl through there. It'll be cold out there, but stay against the wall and don't move, no matter what you see or hear. I'll come back for you when I've dealt with those men."

"Are you going to kill them? You have a gun?"

"No, no gun. Leave it to me. Just go out there and stay close and quiet." Ryska held back the plywood as he crawled obediently through.

Was she going to kill those men? She didn't want to. The Trainers had always been disappointed in her when it came time for the hunting tests. She hated to even kill a rabbit and couldn't imagine taking down a man like the Trainers said they'd have to someday. She hated the hot touch of fresh blood, the metallic taste of it, the slipperiness. She'd hunted out of necessity as she rode the railcars on and off making her away from where the destroyed Lab was to Tynda, hunting just to survive until she'd discovered she could scavenge for wire and scrap to barter for what she needed in the city.

She'd only ever killed one man. The man who'd tried to rape her on her first night in Tynda. She had his cycle now, thinking it, and his life, were fair payment for his crime.

"It's so dark," Toma whispered through the crack as Ryska let the plywood shift back into place. "How will you see?"

"I can't," Ryska said. "Shhh. I'll be back for you."

Freed of having to keep track of the boy, Ryska slipped out of their sanctuary room, carefully mapping out in her memory where she'd left Toma. She crossed the next room, heading back to the hallway and only the shuffle of feet warned her as one of the men stepped through the door, the white blob of his electric torch blinking into her sensor range.

Ryska dove straight at the dark red shape, slashing the torch with her pick-axe. These men might be bigger, stronger and more armed than she, but within the deep darkness of the interior buildings, Ryska had an advantage and she intended to use to its fullest.

The torch crashed to the ground, the white flickering and then going out. This man reacted better than the last had, leaping back and bringing his rifle up. Ryska dropped down and rolled to the side as the Kalashnikov crackled loudly. For a moment her sensors were overwhelmed by the close, loud noise and too-fast-to-track bullets that shook the air as they passed. She wanted to curl her arms around her head and scream.

The flash passed and the world resolved itself back into shades of blue. Ryska forced herself still, watching the red shape creep forward, his breath hissing in her ears. He smelled like sweat and motor oil and his breath carried the bitterness of tabac use on its puffing vibrations as they tickled her whiskers. He toed the area in front of him, searching for his torch, coming within a few feet of her.

Ryska swung her pick-axe into where she thought his knee should be and was rewarded with a scream as he crumpled forward. A sharp blow to his head stopped the next scream and the scent of blood filled her nostrils. She gripped his coat and pulled his body out of the doorway, listening carefully for signs that another was on the way.

Boots running down the hallway. Two sets. *Govno.* Two men. Ryska let her training take over and pushed away the fear. She'd killed one. Now she must kill two more. She could almost hear the Trainers' voices in her head telling her that if she wanted dinner she'd have to find the bunny. *Just a bunny. Just a little blood. Dinner will be good. You can find it. Use your sensors. Let your mind tell the muscles what to do.*

The man had dropped his rifle and it showed up in her sensors in a helpful green color. The programs in her control panel remembered her training, even if she fought to forget. Skull still ringing, she remembered to command to the sensors to identify and dampen their reaction to gunfire.

Ryska plucked up the rifle and swung back to the door as the white of a torch appeared, trailing the red shapes of the men. Her finger found the trigger as the stock rested heavy against her shoulder. Gregr had always told her he found guns easy because he just thought of them as a game. *Just a game. Just a bunny. If you aren't the hunter, you're the rabbit.*

The white shape of the torch flashed into the doorway and Ryska stepped out, opening fire. She heard the bullets hitting the drywall with quick thunks as she blindly sprayed across the area with the red shapes. Then the bullets found bodies and the sound changed, wet thwacks that a sighted ear might not discern. A man cursed loudly and she stepped further into the hallway, firing another burst in his direction. The white blob blinked out. Both red shapes were on the ground, one unmoving, the other groaning and shaking.

Ryska moved cautiously forward. The yellow haze helpfully parted around the men, telling her that they were obstructions in her path and making them look like islands of blood in a sulfur sea. She gagged as the hot smell of ruptured intestines hit her. The man still groaning was gut-shot. She pulled the trigger and fired another burst into his body. *It's the merciful thing to do.*

Stillness. Ryska dropped the rifle, feeling from its weight that the clip was almost spent. She found her pick-axe, a lighter blue, contoured shape on the deep blue of the floor, and put it away in her belt.

No sound of movement or life came from down the hallway. Toma had said six men took him. She'd seen only four within her sensor range out in the square.

If she was lucky, the firefight with Toma's unfortunate rescuers had taken out at least two of the six. Which meant one more man, somewhere. She licked her cold lips and shook the tension out of her hands, torn between grabbing Toma now and heading as quickly as possible for her cycle, and hunting down the other man. She didn't want to kill anyone else if she didn't have to, but she didn't want an armed man at her back, waiting to ambush her.

Ambush. The stairs. She sucked in her breath and crept forward, back down the hall toward where the metal steps were. That's where she'd ambush. Cover the retreat of the men, prevent the boy from slipping away. Gregr and Misha would be so proud of her for thinking like her enemy, for remembering her training.

For remembering them.

It isn't you I wanted to forget, it isn't you I shove away. I just want silence. I want peace. There was no one there to see the words she mouthed, her fingers absently tapping out the code on her thigh.

She hovered at the entrance to the steps, but they were too long for her to sense the full length. Nothing moved that her whiskers could pick up and the yellow haze pointed the way as unobstructed. No tripwires, no broken glass to make noise, nothing that looked like a quick trap set to catch a little boy and his mysterious helper.

Ryska felt a warning twinge as her control panel notified her with a sharp vibration that it was going to need to shut down and collect energy for its battery soon. With all the running and fighting she'd been doing, it would charge pretty quickly, but her sensors would be down, only the touch ones up from her whiskers, no helpful overlay or color mapping to show her the world. She hadn't run it down to nothing in a couple years, but Ryska figured on having ten minutes left, if she was lucky.

She slipped down the stairs carefully, lifting and setting each foot down with minimal noise. Her footfalls sounded hellishly loud in her ears, but her rational mind knew that her hearing was far better than any sighted man's.

There. Red flickered in her sensor range through the pale blue opening into the bottom hallway. The man was lying in wait, hovering behind the protection of the wall. Slowly Ryska slid her satchel off her body with one hand as she pulled out her pick-axe.

The rustling of her bag drew his attention and Ryska threw the sack of wire through the doorway before the man could flick on his torch and expose her. As she'd hoped, he turned the light on the bag, following the sound of movement. Time enough for her to leap forward off the last few steps and tackle him.

He'd half-turned toward her, quicker than she expected and her body slammed into a raised rifle. The metal dug hard into her ribs, knocking the air out of her but her bodyweight and momentum was enough to bring them both crashing backward.

Ryska tried to hit him with the small axe, but she was too tangled, too close. The man started a stream of curses as she rolled away from him and went for the white blob of the torch instead, kicking it in a spinning blur down the hallway until it spun away, out of her sensor range.

"*Sooka*, little cow," the man swore.

Ryska lay still, not daring to move or even breathe as the

man stood, rifle ready. Her ribs ached and she tasted blood where his shoulder had shoved her lip into her teeth, tearing it.

Come toward me, she willed him. *Nothing is here. Just darkness. Come for your light.*

The man fired a burst down the hallway, the bullets flicking by a meter above her head. Then he seemed to stop and listen. Ryska lay flat and breathed shallowly, her heart pounding like an angry fist, so loud that even this man must hear it.

He took a step forward. Listened. Step. Listen. Another step. Ryska tensed, her pick-axe ready. She shoved anyway everything but this moment. She didn't want to be the rabbit.

The red shape stepped closer. In range. She swept up into sitting position, her legs striking out to tangle his forward foot as she swung the pick-axe through the haze of yellow and blue.

The man screamed and brought the rifle down, cracking her hard in the head, but she swung again and shoved herself away, her ears ringing as the control panel pinged again and shut off. The world went dark but the man was in range of her whiskers, the thin, slippery graphene telling his position as he brokenly tried to crawl away and raise his rifle.

Ryska threw herself onto the man, using her sore body to crush the rifle against his chest. Her whiskers brushed his face as she brought the handle of the pick-axe against the man's throat. For a moment, she could almost see his features with the brush of the whiskers. His face felt strangely uneven, his beard prickly. She hadn't touched a human face since the Lab.

Almost with regret, Ryska brought her bodyweight down into the axe handle and crushed the man's throat. Blood sprayed from his mouth, sticking to her cheeks and audibly spattering her goggles. He tried to throw her off and then something cracked in his throat and he stopped moving.

Four dead. Ryska crawled to her feet, tucking the pick-axe into her belt more on habit than through want. She rubbed at her face with one sleeve, glad the blood wouldn't stick to her whiskers. They were finer than human hair. She still wanted a hot shower and an aspirin.

Toma. She had to get him. Get to her cycle. She wasn't sure how long her control panel would keep the sensors off-line. Too long to be useful immediately. She needed to get moving. Luka had compared the kinetic batteries to being like a shark. Stop moving and you'd die. It wasn't quite that dramatic, but without movement, she'd be unable to run the programs that let her function.

And that let her drive the cycle. Ryska decided to deal with that problem as soon as she found Toma.

"Toma?" she called as she finally got back to the room at the end of the upper hallway.

"I'm here." Ryska heard scrabbling as he pried open the plywood and climbed into the room. She guided him carefully past the bodies and had him pick up the still lit electric torch that had slid into another room on the lower floor.

"You have goggles and blood on your face," Toma said.

"Worry about that later." Ryska shrugged. "I need your eyes. I can't see right now, so you'll have to guide us." She explained where she'd left her cycle, trying to find the words to describe the area in a way that Toma could understand.

He was a good guide, patient with her. She only stumbled once. There was no noise other than a soft evening wind rustling the weeds and dead grasses of the square. Ryska moved through the open space, letting her fingers trail along the grasses, anxious for something to orient her in the darkness.

They found her cycle and she helped Toma up in front of her, flicking on the headlamp and praying that it worked since she only bothered with it inside the city where she rarely went at night.

"We'll go slow, but you have to steer," she told Toma.

"You really are blind? You didn't seem blind before."

Ryska lifted her goggles and showed him the empty sockets behind. He gasped but didn't shrink away from her. She felt his head turning back to the front.

"Oh. Okay. I'll steer."

It was a long trip back into the city. Ryska flexed her fingers and wiggled her toes, tapping her tongue against the roof of her mouth, hoping it was enough movement to charge her battery.

"There!" Toma spoke after a long time and steered them left. "Stop," he called and Ryska hit the brakes, letting the cycle idle.

"Public phone?" she asked. She'd told Toma to find her one.

"Yes. I can call papa now. He'll reward you a lot." Toma slid off the cycle but turned and threw his arms around Ryska, surprising her.

She leaned into him, letting his hair tangle in her whiskers for an all-to-brief moment. This close, his hair smelled of lemon soap and wheat and she let herself pretend that she was holding Luka or Misha or...her closed ducts burned again with tears she could never shed.

"Thank you, Ryska," Toma whispered.

"Thank you," she whispered back, not expecting him to understand. She still remembered. She still loved. She'd thought her heart had been buried with the blackened bones beneath the demolished Lab, but she carried it still. It was time to move on and feel again. With Toma's warm arms wrapped tightly around her aching body, Ryska thought that maybe she finally could.

Witness Protection

written by

Louise Herring-Jones

ABOUT THE AUTHOR
Louise Herring-Jones writes mainstream, historical and speculative fiction as well as non-fiction. Her science fiction stories, "Colony Earth Redux" and "Slimed," were published, respectively, in Footprints *(Jay Lake and Eric T. Reynolds, ed., Hadley Rille Books, 2009) and* Northwest Passages *(Cris DiMarco, ed., Windstorm Creative/Orchard House Press 2005). She won the 2009-2010 Charlotte Writer's Club Board Prize for fiction. Her historic baseball article "A Georgia Yankee: The Legend of Johnny Mize" appeared in the 2010* Maple Street Press Yankees Annual *(Cecilia Tan, ed.). She is also a veteran reporter for The Daily Dragon Online (Eugie Foster, ed.). She practices law in Alabama and is an advocate for privacy rights, First Amendment guarantees and other constitutionally protected freedoms. Visit her website at http://www.louiseherring-jones.com.*

Witness Protection

A six-year-old girl had been missing for four hours. She might still be alive, but every minute that passed reduced her chances.

The man handcuffed to the interrogation table had seen Sally Durant alive that afternoon. A gardener employed at Hedgeway Apartments and the only witness to the girl's disappearance, Trent Raymond maintained the grounds and flower beds adjacent to the on-site playground used by tenant children. Earlier that day, Sally returned home from school and played on the swings and slide while her mother watched from the kitchen window. When her mother turned away to reduce the heat under a boiling pot, Sally disappeared. Only Raymond knew what happened, but his story didn't add up.

I blinked my eyes three times to activate my implants. Without a search warrant, the retinal record of the interview could not be used as evidence in court, but I skirted the warrant requirement based on the emergency exception. No one could ever blame Detective Bill Yoko for letting a little girl die over a small constitutional hurdle.

I entered the small room for the third time in as many hours. All I wanted to do was return the girl to her mother. Finding a suspect could wait. I leaned over the table, my palms flat against the gleaming metal surface, and jutted my chin out only inches from the witness's face.

"Last chance to tell the truth, Raymond. No one believes that Sally just vanished."

Raymond shrugged his shoulders. "I told you, man. I was keeping an eye on her like I do any of the complex kids playing alone. One moment she was there, the next second, she was gone."

The corners of my retina blinked blue throughout Raymond's speech. According to all the facial tics measured by the implants' repertoire, the witness told the truth. Red indicated lying and the least subterfuge or uncertainty pushed the signal toward the purple range between red and blue on the retinal spectrum.

"How could that have happened?" I asked, doubting the results of my lie-detecting sensors.

Raymond's face blanched. "I don't know, man," he said, but this time, my retinal indicators flashed red. I jumped forward and spit the next question into the handcuffed man's face.

"She vanished, but you know how, don't you?"

Raymond nodded. I sat down in my chair across the table from the witness.

"If I tell you what I know, will you let me go, no charges? I've been locked to this table for hours," the witness said.

"No promises until I hear what you got to say. I've already got you for lying to investigators. That's at least a year and a grand for every count if the judge slaps you with the max."

"Come on, man. Don't tell me you got them plants?"

I grinned.

Raymond said, "I didn't do anything wrong."

My implants flashed blue, but I pushed again for the information I wanted. "Where is she?"

Raymond held his hands out. "At least, take these cuffs off. I can't feel my fingers."

I keyed in the code to release the magnetic cuffs. The links broke apart. Raymond rubbed his wrists.

"Yesterday," he began, "Sally's father hung around the playground. He sat on the swings, and stared at his ex-wife's windows. Mrs. Durant had left for work earlier, but she told me to call the police if I ever saw her ex." He shook his head and frowned. "But, hey, I'm not gonna rat out a father trying to see his kids."

My implants flashed blue. "Go on," I said. "How long did Durant stay at the playground?"

"Not long. He was gone before Mrs. Durant or Sally came home." Raymond stretched his hands over the table, flexing his fingers repeatedly into fists. "I moved behind the hedges, began trimming. Maybe he thought I couldn't see him."

Purple flashed over my retinas. Was Raymond making up half-truths? "What did he do when he didn't think you were watching?"

"Mr. Durant went over to the sandbox and dug, like he was a kid hisself." Raymond shrugged. "At one point, I thought he dropped his cell into the sand. He said bye as he left the complex. I asked him about his phone. He held it up for me to see, smiling, like he appreciated my concern."

My retinas flashed blue, then purple as Raymond summed up Durant's actions and his encounter with the missing child's father. Some of what he said was true, but some of his story had the taint of falsehood or uncertainty. "Why are you just now telling me this?"

"Look, I don't want to get the guy in trouble. It's bad enough he never gets to see his own kid, but when Sally went missing, she was playing in the sandbox."

Blue, blue, the retinal implants blinked. The guy was telling the truth. "Let's go for a ride, Raymond. You show me where this happened."

"Great," the witness said, and walked around the table. He frowned as I slipped the cuffs back on.

"Protocol." I buzzed for the door to be opened from the outside. "Back to the scene," I told my partner Janet Sinclair. She had observed the interview from behind the two-way mirror that lined the upper wall of the interrogation room.

As Raymond passed, she slipped behind me. "I thought we cleared the father after verifying his alibi and searching his house. You think this guy's onto something?"

"We won't know until we check out the lead," I said.

I pushed Raymond along and Sinclair followed us to the

black sedan parked behind the downtown station.

§

Uniformed patrol officers surrounded the playground and crime scene tape draped from tree to tree to form a circle encompassing the area where Sally had played. Techs scraped the swings for any trace DNA evidence and dusted the slide for prints, but no one seemed to be working the sandbox. Located along the edge of the crime scene, the box lay at the greatest distance from the apartment building where Sally lived with her mother.

"Is that the place?" I asked, pointing and urging Raymond forward.

"That's it. That's where she disappeared," he said to a chorus of blue flashes against my retinas.

My partner Janet hurried across the playground and leapt over the six-inch high wooden enclosure surrounding the sand. She took another step to the center of the box and blinked out-of-sight.

"Holy Moses," I said. "Where'd she go?" I dragged Raymond toward the sandbox and yelled to the nearest uniformed patrolman. "Officer down."

"Take him," I said as the officer rushed to us. I pushed Raymond away, even though my implants registered his protests of innocence as true-blue. I trusted my partner more than I did the emoto-tech built into the retinal sensors.

I drew my stun-gun and followed Janet's path. The playground disappeared in a blend of colors and I stood in another sandbox. Standing a few feet away, Janet leaned by a little girl as she pressed her cell's face. My cell phone vibrated. I holstered my stun-gun and answered, but Janet ended the call when she saw me.

"I think we found her, Bill." She gently pushed the child forward. Tears streaked the little girl's face. "Sally, this is Detective Yoko. He's going to get us home." Janet looked at me, her eyebrows twitching.

"Yeah," I said, trying to sound confident. "Sally, do you want to help me find something in the sand? I think there's a little box that might help us."

Sally nodded and the three of us knelt down and picked through the sand until we found a small black metal box about the size of a mobile phone.

"Janet, you used to be in the military, right?

My partner nodded as I handed her the phone. She looked at the smooth plastic sides. "If this is doing what I think, it's a stealth device, kind of a portable hidey-hole for spies. Uses cameras, prisms, and who knows whatever new gizmos the intel agencies have developed, maybe even a force field."

I still had my retinal sensors on. Janet's assessment read blue to violet. "Do you know how to turn it off?" I asked.

She held the box up and turned it over and inspected each side. "Nope, can't say that I do, but if you'll back me, I think I can put it out of commission." She pulled her stun-gun off her belt and held it against the box with its probes on either side of the device. She hit the stun and the current arced around the box. The stealth shield fell away. We were back in the playground. Sally ran to her mother.

§

We drove Code Two to Durant's house on the other side of town with back-up following. When we arrived, the door hung open on its hinges. We sent one uniform to cover the back and Janet led the way inside with her pistol drawn. I followed. But someone had already wrecked the place and left. If Durant had been home then, he had long since left the building.

Janet found an employee badge tossed into a far corner of the bedroom closet. "Unbroken Circle Technologies," she read. "I've heard of that place."

"Not me," I said. "Any idea what they do?"

"Naw, just another high-tech think tank. Probably where Durant got the stealth device."

"Good guess," I said, my retinas flashing blue and matching the confidence I felt in the lead. I pulled out my phone and drew up the search warrant we would need on its digital display. I sent the warrant to Janet's phone and the emergency number I had for the presiding judge. One video-conference later, we held digitally signed search and arrest warrants fresh out of the sedan's onboard laser printer. We got back into the cars and drove to Unbroken Circle Tech. Janet called in for more back-up to meet us there.

§

We drove down roads in the research complex, each named for a famous scientist, until we got to Tesla Boulevard. Three patrol cars and a SWAT wagon followed our sedan. We pushed through the glass doors into Unbroken Circle's building with a small army behind us. Three security guards stood up from a desk just beyond the door.

"You can't come in here. Restricted access, top secret only," the middle guard yelled.

"Here's my access," I said, tossing the search warrant on the desk. "We have reason to believe that your technology was used in a kidnapping."

The head guard tossed the warrant back at my chest. "Not on my watch, buddy," he said.

I stepped to his left and he stuck out his hand to stop me. "You're not going through."

Janet pulled her stun-gun and pressed it against the right side of the man's neck. He dropped like a rock. The other guards rushed us, but the SWAT team fired a barrage of stun-shotguns. Stun bullets hit the guards' suits and hung there. The guard closest to me grabbed a bullet stuck on his suit. Electric current arced within the transparent casing of the clinging bullet and that guard also fell. The third guard raised his hands as he was surrounded by the SWAT team.

I held up the stealth device from the sandbox to the remaining guard. "Where can I find these?" I asked.

He mumbled something, but a prod from the butt of one of the shot-guns encouraged him to talk. "Third floor," he answered. "Covert support lab."

Janet led the way to the elevator. We took three SWAT ninjas with us and left the rest of the team and the uniforms to hold the guards and secure the building's perimeter. "How you liking your implants, Bill?" the head ninja asked, a fellow I knew from a cop bar downtown.

"Doing great so far, thanks. How about you?" I asked.

"New helmets just came in. Thermal sensors let us see people through walls. We'll find your bad guys for you."

"No doubt," Janet added as the elevator chime rang three times for our destination floor.

The doors slid open and our ninjas stepped out first, looking each way with their visors in place. The head guy waved to us and we followed him to the right. About half-way down the hall, the label "COVERT SUPPORT" marked one of the doors. The SWAT guys pointed their shotguns. I yelled "Police." When no one answered, I motioned to the team and they broke the door down.

The lab was lined from floor to ceiling with every type of weapon used in modern police work and a number that I didn't recognize. The SWAT ninjas moved ahead of us to the far end of the lab. Three men sat around a table with a fourth man I already knew on sight, Ike Durant, Sally's father. Durant looked like an overgrown owl with two bruised and blackened eyes and his hair mussed into points.

"Gentlemen." A tall man with graying hair stood up from the table. "Welcome to our facility. I take it the guards put up enough of a fuss that we won't have any trouble with security clearance issues?"

"Sir, I don't know you, but I'm Bill Yoko," I said. I handed him the warrant. "We are here to search for any weapons or other devices used in the kidnapping of a child earlier today. And since Mr. Durant is here, I also have a warrant for his arrest." I handed the second warrant to Durant. I turned back to the gray-haired man. "I'll need your name for receipt of service," I added.

"No problem with the name, but I'm afraid you can't search our laboratories. I'm George Morgan, the CEO of UCT. These two gentlemen are your federal counterparts and they're questioning Mr. Durant about the theft of some rather valuable equipment from our lab. Until they find the missing device, I'm afraid Mr. Durant will be otherwise engaged."

I held up the stealth box we'd taken from the sandbox. "You mean this device?" When Morgan stepped forward, I held the box away from him. "We're holding this as evidence in the kidnapping of Sally Durant. But since now you know where it is, we'll just take Mr. Durant out of here, after we execute our search and seize whatever evidence we may need for court."

"Seize evidence? You're not taking anything," Morgan grumbled. "And that box is company property."

My implants flashed red. I laughed. "I'm not sure it works anymore," I said. "My partner had to apply her stun-gun to free us and little Sally. But we'll need a working model for our case against Durant."

The two other men, each dressed in gray suits, white shirts and dark ties, had the glimmer of retinal implants sparkling in their eyes. One shook his head. "I'm afraid we're going to have to pull rank on you, Detective Yoko. The device you've taken illegally is government property and we're federal agents."

My implant flashed purple. "Let's see a badge," I said. "What are you, FBI, CIA, Homeland Security?"

The man flipped a wallet opened. The federal seal shone

out from his badge, but no agency emblem appeared on either the badge or his ID card.

"Agent Duerr," I read. "What's your agency?"

"Let's just say we're federal agents at large, ghosts to shadow spooks. Strictly need-to-know, Detective, and you don't need to know any more than we'll give up Durant when we're finished here and that device in your hand isn't going anywhere."

Janet reached over and held my arm before I could answer. "One minute," I said. "I need to confer with my partner." We walked back through the lab doors, but left our ninjas standing over the men in the lab.

"Remember the interview with Raymond?" Janet asked. "Durant didn't have any visitation with his daughter. I think he went off the deep end and took something he wasn't supposed to have and we weren't supposed to see."

"The stealth device?" I asked.

"Yes, and one with a force field to boot. We know why Durant took it, to see his kid. I'm betting he's no spy and they want that device back. Let's do a trade and get the man out of here before they kill him or, worse, ship him off to some hellhole where he'll never be found."

"How do I know he's not a spy?"

"Those guys have retinal implants, too. They know he's telling them the truth, but they want a scapegoat. They're trying to beat a confession out of him."

"I guess I could ask him?"

"Isn't that what lie detection is all about?" Janet snorted at me and led the way back into the lab.

#

My partner, right again, proved to me that day that sometimes solid detective skills trumped the latest equipment. The feds wanted that device more than they wanted Durant, but Janet wasn't satisfied. Durant plead guilty to a misdemeanor for interference with his ex-wife's custody of their daughter and Janet got him into the state witness protection program over the felony breaking and entering of his home by the ghosts that shadowed the spooks. The unnamed federal agency never claimed the work at Durant's home as a lawful search. After several trips to a plastic surgeon, Durant went to work for the state police developing investigative technology. And the witness protection provisions included family contact, so Durant finally got visits with his daughter.

About a month after Durant shipped out to the state's new ultra-secret, anti-crime technology center, Janet brought coffee and doughnuts into the office.

"What are these for?" I asked.

"Just thought you needed to feel the love," she said.

"For what?

"For backing me up on the Durant case. I never thought I'd be putting a would-be felon into our witness protection to keep him safe from the feds."

My retinal implants flashed blue. "Got any chocolate-covered crullers hidden in that bag?" I asked.

"No," Janet said as my implants changed to red.

Stage Presence, Baby

written by

E.M. Schadegg

ABOUT THE AUTHOR
E.M. Schadegg is a science-fiction writer living in Maryland with her long-time honey and their two children. She loves notebooks, all types, and is always excited to see what world she'll find hidden within the recesses of the newest one. Her family fuels the addiction by giving her more. She is also a winner of the Writers of the Future Contest *(Vol. 28) under her fantasy pen name, Marie Croke.*

Stage Presence, Baby

At least he waited until the end of the show instead of accosting me during a frail ten minute program check. I might have done something disastrous then. Either on stage or behind the scenes.

Crossing my arms, I didn't even bother shaking my head at his bold presumption. "I don't sing for aliens."

He flinched. Or rather, his outward appearance flinched. Angs were nothing like the angels they attempted to mimic.

"You'd have the best coder," he said. His voice held a soft quality to it. Not his real voice. One he chose. Normally Angs liked to be heard resoundingly by all around them. This Ang had transmitted an almost demure attitude.

I narrowed my eyes in suspicion. "You mean I'd look like an angel, oh?"

The tips of his wings shivered then. They turned towards me, catching the backstage light in such a way my eyes stung. I toned the gloss down a bit so my eyes wouldn't water and make me look a fool. Most people didn't have that luxury. Most people thought what they saw was reality. Angs liked it that way. Liked seeing the dropped reverent gazes.

"Well," he said, a nervous tremble echoing from his VocTrans. A base model, not even as well designed as my own, made to take over with prerecorded syllables if it detected a fluctuation in my voice while I performed. "Not exactly."

My blood chilled at the words. I'd thought he'd meant heading up to the Greens where the Angs liked to gamble. A lot of performers tried to make it there, tried to get an Ang sponsor. I'd shied away, first out of fear, then out of anger.

"No," I said. I saw the flicker of a violet message at the bottom of my screen, registering that my VocTrans had taken over for the one syllable.

Angry now that the Ang had startled me so, I spun around, letting my projected dress swirl.

"Please. At least, talk to me. I'm here because of *you*, not what you do."

I almost turned back, the fact that an Ang had actually said please to me made me curious. But we all know what they say about that. So I continued on, making tracks for my agent.

"Sincere!"

I let him scream. His voice cracking brokenly, causing heads to turn. Maybe I just liked the feeling of power. Finally, after a life living under the Ang, I had one flustered.

§

A week later, I began to regret my rash actions.

"Come on, baby, Greens is the biggest joint in the city. Any star but the rappers down on Memphis Street would *kill* for this," said Chris. They would. It'd happened before. "And obviously they wanted you, sending one of their own after you like that."

Flattery had never gotten him anywhere, so why he used it now disturbed me. I'd been seriously reconsidering whether he was worth twenty percent and this gave him another check under the con side of having him around.

"Cancel."

His mouth dropped. "Baby, but...I can't do that, sweetheart."

I shrugged and picked up my tea, letting its scent fill my nose, my lungs. I had long since stopped reacting to the names. If I complained, he smiled brighter and used them more often. So instead I ignored them. Over time people realized it meant nothing.

People meaning humans. I'd never worked with Angs before. They'd have no experience to draw from, no knowledge that they made their bookings directly through *me*, not him.

"So trade it with Hemi Gable or PrinCess."

"PrinCess? You can't be serious, half her work is about teenage angst. The Angels wouldn't go for that."

"Angs," I correctly automatically. Some idiot had supplied the 'el' when the Angs had first started hacking into our transmissions, morphing their technology with ours. They'd run with it, as any good dictator would. We're the idiots for allowing it.

"Angels."

"Doesn't matter," I said. "I'm not going. I don't really care what you do to fix your booking problem."

"That's irresponsible of you and it'll look bad, not on me, but on you. Bad publicity, baby."

"I know how to deal with the press," I said softly, taking a sip of my tea.

"Fuck, baby, if I have to I'll set up a holo of you."

I laughed in his face, which made him even angrier. "You think they won't know the difference, Chris? Go ahead and do that. Explain to them why you tried to run a scam. My word will hold more weight."

It hadn't always been so. There'd been times I'd followed his lead, fuming, with no control over the decisions made. Those times had come and gone and he just hadn't realized it yet.

Watching him storm off, his skin a shade too bright to be real, his blonde locks without an ounce of frizz of reality, I wondered how I'd ever thought him attractive when he'd first offered to help me become a star.

He'd made a few phone calls, but he'd not made me great. That I'd done myself. On the stage, with my own songs. With my own programs. It was all about stage presence.

And then I'd found out the truth about the Angs, about the interstates and New Baltimore. I put the tea back down at the memory.

All I'd wanted was an airplane. A real airplane to take me to Richmond for a concert. Not the hovers that could barely sit a few feet off the ground or the old rails hooked into their tracks.

I'd pitched a fit. The one fit I ever remember throwing. The mags would have eaten it up if they'd heard of it. Telling the city and all beyond just how much a diva I truly was. No real classy lady here, they'd have said.

But they didn't find out, because the Angs would have been furious. The one news reporter who'd slipped in had been found dead the next day. Blood pumped full of narcotics.

I moved to the window, stepped out on my balcony and looked up at the view. Felt the sun upon my face, the wind lifting the ends of my hair. Could see for miles, across the city and beyond.

Then, slowly, I blocked the transmissions, putting in codes I'd learned by heart when the Angs finally had to show me. They hadn't counted on a performer's memory. All the notes, all the words I had to memorize and they thought I couldn't remember a few number sequences.

The bright blue sky faded. The birds became shadows before disappearing altogether. The darkness of the ground beyond seemed even more bleak today. Casting the city in a deeper haze of filth. Except for the high streets.

My gaze lingered on those streets. I could see the outline of the Greens from here. See the line of the groundscrapers, their tops embedded into and going through to the surface above. Everyone else called them skyscrapers. The immense homes of the Angs. The only beings free to see real sky.

And that's the thought that made me reconsider. If that Ang had been right, then he'd meant for me to perform up *there*. Where I'd see real sky. Hear real birds. Smell the scent of flowers on the wind. Wind brought from air currents of the earth, not fans and motors running silently about the city, embedded in the dirt walls of the outer perimeter.

I was tempted. Sorely tempted.

I closed my eyes tight and recaptured the trans, waiting until I saw the scrolling messages announcing their presence in my eyelids before opening them again. There, the city felt normal again. Less constricting. The sky bright, the sun a gorgeous ball in the sky. The brick and metal sides of the buildings bright and clean.

In one half of my cornea's view screen I called up the list of my stage presences. This one had long blue hair, slightly deeper set eyes. That one had a darker shade of skin, so black I contrasted with the bright pinks of my outfits. Another held a frail hint of an angel's wings, flecked with silver and black, mocking the Angs' perfect glossy white wings with the truth of reality.

None had more than one or two aspects of who I was changed. Nothing too huge, nothing too drastic. I made sure of that. All of them were intrinsically Sincere. Me.

To create a presence so unlike me, to learn how to move so that my body felt as an Ang's...

It disgusted me...and intrigued me.

Calling up the files from when I'd met the Ang after the concert, I studied his trans feeds. There was a bit there to differentiate him. Something to trace.

§

"I've been thinking about a concert at the Greens," I said by way of greeting. It served a two-fold purpose, despite its untruth. One, to smooth over reactions around me in the restaurant, giving me a reason to be conversing with an Ang. And two, to let him know I was going to be more receptive today.

"I'd heard," he said as I slipped in the seat opposite of him.

His wings were folded back, less of a distraction in such a crowded place. Odd behavior for an Ang.

"And?" I asked.

"You can sing where you like, Sincere." He didn't sound as if he wanted me to though. Maybe he just knew about my stubbornness.

"You are giving me permission?" I asked, arching my brow in amusement.

He shook his head. "I'm not sure anyone could do that. You'll do what you wish."

"The Angs could order me to."

He shook his head again. "I doubt it. Your world runs through entertainment. People react to it fiercely. Riot when things don't go their way in a game or a concert."

How well I knew. I could almost taste the pounding of a crowd's shouts, screaming for more, their voices pulsing in my blood. Flicking my gaze to the corner of my eye-screen I saw a tiny thumbnail of a recorded moment moving there, called up by my memory. I shut it down. I had no time for emotion right now.

"So," I said with a smile, "am I going to have to come up with a name for you as is our way, or are you sure enough in yourself you can give me your real one?"

He hesitated, but only for a fraction of a second. "The best human interpretation is Neils."

I was shocked, had already been running through a

few things I could call him in my head. Hiding the feeling, I immediately ran the name through my own limited translator. It was a hack and the vocabulary and population listing was small, the program created by a half-dozen alien obsessors trying to find a way into the Angs' good graces. It hadn't worked, of course, but I hadn't bothered discovering what had happened to them.

The name didn't ping on anything. Not surprising, but it'd been worth a try.

"Neils," I said, trying the name out. It seemed to fit with his quiet manner. No hard ending, no unpronounceable syllables. "What exactly are you proposing? You and I both know that a human beyond the scrapers would be unheard of."

"Wait." Neils' gaze wandered casually about the restaurant, as if worried about the visual and audio feeds. But he shouldn't be. Any Ang could overlay transmissions, making the feeds see and record one thing while the people saw another, and neither had to be the truth. Targeted realities. They were experts at it. One reason why most of the city, most of every city, believed they truly were angels from another planet.

A sudden upsweeping upon my screen, glaring red, startled me so badly I almost knocked over my water glass. *A hack, he's hacking me.* I started to shut everything down, to see only the basics of what existed around me. I might be able to design amazing stage presence, but I'd never been fast at it. The garbled red words kept jumping up my screen until, blinking once, they disappeared, leaving only a warning signal scrolling across the bottom of my screen.

"You hacked me," I said accusingly, trying to keep my

hands from shaking.

"I apologize. I only needed to access your VocTrans. I swear I didn't touch your files."

"Why?" I demanded as I began a search regardless of what he said. I realized my voice had shook on the syllable and instantly double-checked to make sure my VocTrans was working. It was. And not just working, working as hard as it'd been the day I'd given an outside concert down in Low Norfolk. I'd had a cold, my voice completely gone. I began to relax as my search came up empty. No corrupted files, not even a whisper of activity anywhere.

"To give the people around us and the audio feeds something to record."

I could have checked to see what kind of conversation he was having the VocTrans relay, but I didn't bother. I could check it over later. If Neils was willing to do it, then he wasn't just trying to hide something from my people, he was also trying to hide it from his own.

"So we can talk freely?" I asked.

He nodded, slowly, eyes reflecting relief. An all too human-like relief.

"So," I said, spreading my hands out, but only slightly, wanting my visual to make sense with whatever audio Neils had being transmitted. "What makes you think Angs would like my singing?"

"It's not your singing. It's your presence. I've been to your concerts, seen the way you capture the crowd, holding them by their jugulars until *you* want them to be free. Your singing is average, the words average, all done better by other human singers. But humanity lives off of entertainment. Thrives off it. Moves and reacts to it."

I drummed my fingers on the tablecloth, holding annoyance in check at his insult. His flattery didn't have the same vibe that Chris' had. Neils spoke with excitement, not for me, for something greater that he thought I could be part of.

"I'm with you so far," I said, nodding for him to go on.

He hesitated again, biting his lower lip. Behavior so human-like it scared me. A sudden anxiety came over me then and I purposely blocked his visual transmission. His wings faded into transparency, letting me see the table behind him. His dark hair, usually falling almost into his eyes, shortened, sinking into a thinner head, a more oblong head. The hand resting upon the table shaded darker, becoming a mottled grey and black, as it twisted into something more akin to a tentacle.

I immediately opened the trans back up, in time to see a startled expression cross his human skin, wingtips fluttering lightly. He'd coded his appearance to react to his real emotions. For himself? For me?

"Satisfied?" asked Neils.

I shrugged, trying not to announce how disturbed I was that he was connected to my feeds enough he could tell when I blocked something. He'd probably known I'd searched my files earlier as well.

"When Angs first came to Earth, we thought we were different. Better than you by the space of a wide margin. Where you obsessed over entertainment and leisure activities, we obsessed with expansion, in both technology and in space. We eagerly learned your race's tricks and expanded upon them with our own advances."

"I'm aware of history," I said in a bored tone, fingers rapping harder, individual, against the table. Neils stared at them.

"We thought we were better."

My index finger froze in midair. "Thought?"

Neils looked up at me. "Thought. Now we know better, it's just most of us won't admit it. Our expansion, our immersion in your technology was all our own form of entertainment. We discovered even more watching your people create, realized that we don't just have to find what is already in existence, but can create spectacles that aren't real to provoke our imagination."

"Interesting," I whispered. "But what exactly does it have to do with me?"

"We have our own singers now, you know."

I hadn't known. It wasn't as if we had Angs down here performing for us. In fact, now that I thought about it, there weren't any Angs performing in the Greens either, and yet they booked human after human, from singers to comedians, circus troupes to orchestras. I'd even heard a children's talent show had gone on there once, though I didn't know how much truth there had been to that rumor.

"They stole what they heard from the Greens at first," said Neils, "Then they mimicked. A few are now popping up here and there who are actually creating their own work and are getting a decent reception up above. Your culture has had such a tremendous impact on our own."

I laughed then. "So you want me to sell you some programs?" I asked. Stage presence, he'd said. "Make some nice little Ang band or wannabe pop star look good when they take to the stage with butterflies and relaxers. And you thought, great, there's a singer down there who knows the truth who might be willing to jump on board if we let her perform for us. Sorry, I don't program Ang's presences. Ever."

Neils shook his head. "No, you don't understand."

The frailty in his voice stopped me from rising.

"My people pretend to be *human* to perform up there."

I know my jaw dropped. I could have transmitted a visual so it didn't show, but I didn't. The shock had gone all the way to my bones. Even the helpful little feed in the bottom of my screen faded when my mind blanked out for the moment.

"What? Why?" I asked.

A sigh came from Neils' VocTrans. "Why do teens insist on striped skin? Why do women augment their chests? Why do people constantly change their appeared wardrobe despite the temperature never changing?"

"So you're saying it's a fad." I knew that wasn't what he meant, but I wanted to hear him say it regardless.

Neils frowned. "Not a fad, no. That word translates into a shortened period of time. This has been going on for years now. And before that it started in other things. Interpersonal games with involving story-lines...you do know that half the people playing over the networks are Angs, right?"

I hadn't. The way they'd kept themselves away I had assumed they'd either have their own systems, or none at all. But

I guess we weren't quite as separated as they'd like us to believe.

He leaned over the table, eyes searching mine. Almost as if he'd be able to communicate effectively despite me knowing that his real eyes were embedded in his skin and covered with a thin film that made reading them almost impossible for a human.

"There's some of us who realize that we aren't so much better. That humans have an amazing imaginative quality that spurs your technological advances along faster than we'd thought possible. If you compared how long your culture took to discover things compared to ours...it's simply downright impressive. We want our people to mingle further, not simply in the digital world, or hidden in the one or two luxury casinos like the Greens. We want your abilities to rub off on us."

He said *us* in a manner that worried me. It could have been unconscious, simply a racial them versus us. But it could have been something else.

I dropped my blocks again and examined him once more without his human appearance. He truly had lurched partway over the table, mottled body tense. Worried? Annoyed? I wasn't versed in Ang body language. None of us were.

He could be working for an agency. Possibly governmental, possibly private. Only his motives over time might show which, and that meant working with him.

Finally what Neils was asking dawned upon me. "So when you asked me to sing, you didn't mean just once. Not some quick jaunt to the surface to be a passing fancy dancing like a puppet on your stages. You want me to pretend to be one of you."

His body slouched back in the chair and he lifted the

tentacle-hand slightly, the end wavering. I didn't know what that meant either, but I hadn't blocked his audio projection.

"Essentially. We want you to be a star. Show our half of this world exactly how much they could benefit from learning among you. We have the ability to give you a basic code underneath your usual projections to make you look inherently Ang. No one will be able to block it any more than the average human can block our appearances. You'd do everything as you normally do, but above ground."

I let his angelic gaze filter in once more so I could read him more effectively. "And what happens then? Will the truth come out about your natures? How you are not God Almighty's creatures, but rather simple beings who shoved us underneath the ground to claim our surface as your own? That we'd begin to see more equality?"

Neils looked down. Ashamed? No, sad. "I'd like to think so," he said.

And whatever else he might have said, I believed him then. Whatever agency he might be working for wouldn't go for it, but he did. It might be enough to have an Ang mostly on my side. It'd have to be enough.

I started my drumming back up, the silverware clinging together with every tap of my index finger. He waited patiently, quiet and still. The difference between him and Chris gave me goose bumps up my arms. My fingers paused again as I realized if I took him up on his offer I'd be starting all over again. From the bottom, working my way up.

I glanced around, at the people in the restaurant. Some had

been giving me furtive looks. Glances that spoke of admiration, jealousy, excitement. Lost in their false world of fallen angels and fake suns.

It didn't have to be that way though.

I looked back at Neils. He still waited. Patiently.

"One condition."

He motioned for me to go on, obviously expecting the demand.

"I keep my concert schedules here as well. We pretend my above personae is simply mimicking myself and I go below to study her."

"Are you sure?" Neils asked, brow furrowed slightly, but from worry, not annoyance. "It'd be easy enough to stage a death."

Of course it would be. Keep me stuck, unable to go back to the life I'd had. I may have taken him up on that offer once, long ago, but I was no longer a naive street-singer boning for a chance to succeed.

I shook my head slowly, an amused smirk growing upon my face. "I keep myself and I perform for you...for double my normal concert fee. And I'll want to meet with the Ang in charge of your agency."

He licked his lips, but the excitement reflecting in his eyes didn't dim. Then he nodded. "Yes, of course, those are easy to accommodate. I'll have the preliminary contract drafted up. You do understand it'll have to be confidential, correct?"

Yes, he seemed to be the pure hearted one. Maybe that's why they'd sent him. I didn't know and didn't care. I'd be using him and whoever was in charge.

I needed to brush up on my Ang knowledge though. Real Ang knowledge, not the glossy winged angels they pretended to be. Then I'd be in business for real. *Stage presence, baby*, as Chris would put it.

The thought of selling an Ang program exhilarated me, not the monies, but the possibilities. How long before there were humans living above, among the Ang? Not long if I kept my head on straight. Kept my eyes open and kept learning.

"I understand," I said. Then I blocked his beautiful winged appearance from my sight, letting his mottled alien form fill my vision. I'd start today. "Now that that's settled, why don't you remove your hack and tell me about yourself."

He did, obviously too focused on excitement over my agreement. I ran a scan immediately, searching, then searching again for anything left within my files.

Nothing.

I smiled brightly at him. "So, Neils, who's your favorite human singer? And don't say me, flattery doesn't get you far in my good graces." I spoke in an engaging manner, waiting for him to show me an Ang tell for excitement.

The film over his eyes grew brighter as he responded and I could feel the wind under the table from one of his tentacles sweeping cross-wise in front of me. I filed the information away, encrypted and password protected.

§

I let Neils come up with my new name. Sing. He said it was the human form of a real name for them. Hard end. I believed him. I read their mags where they said admiringly how I'd studied deeply of human culture and language before taking to the stage for the first time. It was the truth, in a way.

Neils gave me a thumbs up before I climbed the ladder.

Stepping out upon the stage, onto a thin walkway projecting a cloudy obscuration, I looked as if I walked on air. I made my wings flap behind me, blowing long blue-green hair in the wind they created.

The lights blinded me, as they always did, making it difficult to see the Angs in all their true forms. Their voices though, raised in shouts, unintelligible, were familiar. Heart speeding, blood pulsing in unison with their excitement, I raised my arm and swept it out to encompass everyone gathered.

Then I began to sing, my presence exploding to take over the entire stage, the program designed to hold them to me, belong to me until I let them finally breathe on their own.

I could hear Neils' promises to help me in the back of my mind, telling me how he'd make me a star all over again. On the surface, where the sky still shone bright and the birds sang. Where my people had once ruled. I smiled and my presence smiled all the brighter, making the crowd shout, thinking it was for them.

He could make a few phone calls.

I would make me great.

And when I had billions of Angs in love with me, I'd show them the true power and sway of pure, unadulterated entertainment.

Gift Horses

written by

K.E. Abel

ABOUT THE AUTHOR
A voracious reader ever since teaching herself at the age of three, she is known for reading everything in her path, but has always returned to science fiction and fantasy. Her varied and diverse hobbies include (but are certainly not limited to): gardening, climbing, photography, knitting, karate, jam and soap making and, of course, writing.

In 2011 she embarked on a 100 Book Challenge, inspired by the Facebook BBC meme/myth. You can join in, or check progress at her official website and blog: www.randomsynapses.ca. Cyberstalkers can also find her @randomsynapses (Twitter).

She currently lives near Vancouver, British Columbia and can generally be found wearing her signature mismatched socks. Her writing space is shared with her spouse, two sleepy leopard geckos and a collection of stuffed dragons. Although she has been making up tales her entire life, especially why her school work wasn't finished, this is her first published story.

Gift Horses

The city had certainly changed since the last time she was there, Sasha thought as she glanced up at the skyscrapers around her. She blinked and an overlay of what the city had looked like ten years before appeared in front of her eyes, the ghostly imprint over each building and street as she turned around. Many of the smaller buildings had been replaced by towers over one-hundred stories high and it seemed cleaner as well. A slight squint with her left eye and the overlays vanished, replaced with a blue line leading her to the shop.

Other pedestrians hurried along the treed sidewalk, going in different directions. Sasha was fascinated by the archaic idea of free flowing sidewalks, being used to the uni-directional walkways. Few of the walkers seemed to be in any danger of bumping into their fellow commuters, despite being distracted. Many of the pedestrians made slight movements as they walked: hand and facial tics, soft fingertip brushes over different parts of their skin and clothing as they accessed the virtual world around them. Sasha followed the gaze of several people toward the city's main OverSight building and turned on her view. What had been a blank, silver building suddenly came alive with recent citizen alerts for suspected criminals floating around the outside of it. A smaller band of screens above the photographs had running updates on an ongoing investigation in some suspicious explosions in an OverSight development centre. Turning away from the building, she continued toward the shop.

An old fashioned bell chimed over the door as Sasha entered the shop. She was always looking for vintage CyChips, and she had heard that this was one of the better stores in the city. Most of the newer CyPackets were available through a virtual store in her interface, but some of the older and higher memory ones were only available in physical chip form.

Looking through the black wire racks, she adjusted her OverSight and information instantly appeared in her view. Dates, titles and writer's credits pointed to the different boxes as she focused on them. One in the back of a rack caught her eye. She had been looking for an in depth plant and animal encyclopedia for a few months now, but there wasn't a lot of demand for them. She took it from the rack and flipped it over. It wasn't a publisher she was familiar with, but according to her OverSight, they had been around for decades, so it was likely decent quality.

Sasha took the CyChip up to the front counter. The owner glanced at it as she ran her finger across the bar code and the total flashed in front of Sasha's eyes. Sasha touched her wrist and the money was transferred from her balance.

"Will you be able to run this one?" the owner asked, obviously taking her age into account. "It doesn't interface with the newer OverSights directly." More recent OverSight implants had different jacks and some of the older chips wouldn't work with them, but Sasha had received a fully integrated system before she had been born. There were silvery threads throughout her entire neurosystem, giving her a level of control that was unheard of with the older jacks or the newer, safer ones. She could use physical jacks, and could run specialized controls with every part of her body.

"I've got an adaptor. Thanks."

Sasha left, nearly running into a vaguely familiar man she thought she recognized from a seminar earlier that morning, coming in through the front door. She nodded briefly, and narrowed her left eye bringing up a thin green line to guide her back to her hotel.

Arriving back at her quietly bland room, Sasha sat on the bed, deliberating. She took a drink from the glass of ice water on the desk beside her. She still had another three hours before her next seminar, a panel she was chairing on the ethics of full neural integration. That would be plenty of time to upload her new CyChip, play with it a little and unslot it again when it was time to go to her panel. With a quick thumb flick, she checked how much space was left in her OverSight and, finding that there was plenty for the new chip without having to delete and reinstall any other packets, decided to play with it a little.

Breaking the seal of the packet with her thumbnail, the wrapping shrank and disintegrated into a few specks of dust that quickly dissipated into the room. She opened the flesh-tinted control panel she'd had installed on the inside of her left wrist. Sasha attached the adaptor she took from her suitcase to one of the wrist ports that were connected to the main OverSight unit. The main unit was integrated behind her spine near her tailbone. She appreciated the thought that her parents had when they put it in a less obtrusive spot than the typical base of neck or behind the ear, but it was certainly a more awkward place to attach cables to.

With the ease of long practice, Sasha snapped open the CyChip, exposing the contact point and plugged it into the end of the adaptor cord. With her thumb, she held down the power switch and the chip lit up, glowing softly.

Sasha frowned slightly. The expected first flood of information hadn't come. Normally when an older CyChip was first installed there would be a stream of images and text for several seconds, far too quickly for the human brain to process more than one in ten thousand or so, as the data integrated with the full body network. Many people found it unpleasant, almost like a muscle cramp in the brain, but Sasha had always enjoyed the slight tingling pain, comparing it to the ache after exercise. Standing, she was surprised to feel her physical muscles aching slightly. They were stiff, as if she had been in one position for a long period of time. An unobtrusive, yet insistent peal was sounding in her mind. With a movement of her tongue, Sasha answered her internal phone.

"Ms. Laren?" A smiling woman's face appeared at the edge of Sasha's vision.

"Yes?" Her throat was dry and she took a sip of the warm water in the glass beside her.

"The organizers are wondering if you will be able to attend your panel today," she said.

Sasha blinked, and a small digital clock appeared under the projection of the woman. It had been almost three and a half hours since she had plugged into the CyChip. "Yes, I'll be right there. Please let them know."

The woman nodded and she faded out as the connection broke. Cursing, Sasha quickly popped the adapter cord out of her wrist jack and closed the panel face. No time to change. She ran her fingers through her short, blond hair, hoping to tousle it into something resembling an intentional style. Her youth and attractiveness often seemed to be a mark against her when attending these types of events, and now her tardiness would be yet another black spot for her detractors to use. Being taken seriously was a frequent problem. She tossed the cable and still-attached CyChip onto the bed, deciding that she would return the defective software sometime before her week-long trip was over.

Leaving her room, Sasha closed the door behind her and headed to the bank of elevators covering the entire wall at the end of the hallway. An empty elevator arrived quickly. She waved her hand in front of the control panel and the elevator began to drop to the floor she needed. She tried to straighten her clothes in the mirrored wall, having given up on her hair. The elevator was silent as it moved swiftly down dozens of levels, arriving with an inconspicuous and faintly apologetic hiss as the doors opened to a richly decorated floor. The appearance of this area was in great contrast to the beige budget rooms that were on Sasha's floor. A thick, dark green carpet covered the floor with contrasting wall paper and small alcoves every six meters or so with art tucked back in them. Vases, paintings and sculpture filled the spaces and the occasional empty space had a silvery panel at the back where the inclined could turn their OverSight and see a modern creation or a reproduction of an ancient piece of art in fully realized color and shape. Sasha didn't have time to admire the art but she quickly tuned her OverSight to tell her which room was the right one.

A sudden barrage of information made her gasp. Suddenly there were different colored glowing lines pointing to everything within her field of vision with information scrolling faster than she could read. Her entire field of vision lit up to the point where she couldn't see anything of the real world. Every available space was filled with a blinding and bewildering array of words connecting everything to each other. Even having exposure to the availability of communications provided by her full body neural network, she was overwhelmed by the sudden blow to her nervous system. Her legs sagged under her and she grabbed the edge of a shelf in one of the alcoves for support. Fortunately it was an OverSight display and didn't have any physical objects for her to damage. She could see small black spots out of the corners of her eyes, growing larger as the information overload continued. She tried to switch her OverSight off, first mentally then physically, using her thumb against her right earlobe. Closing her eyes seemed to bring some relief, cutting off the images that insisted on being categorized and organized and immediately viewed. There was no priority to any of the things she was seeing and there didn't seem to be any way for her to filter them out.

Even blocking out the visual stimulation didn't help for long. Her heartrate and blood pressure, both unsurprisingly elevated, appeared on the inside of her eyelids, as did the lyrics, credits and music video for the N-Pop song playing over the speakers in the alcove she was leaning in. Sasha jerked away as her elbow brushed against the OverSight screen, overlaying the interpretive dance display over the music video in a disjointed, jerky full screen display, complete with all of the alternate takes, out takes and director's commentary running simultaneously. She slowly slid to the floor, hands covering her ears. Normally incidental movement didn't cause her OverSight to run; she needed to have intent behind her commands, but for some reason every movement was causing the system to react as if she were telling it to seek out information and display it.

Information about someone lit up her vision; photograph, name, age, weight, height, medical history, credit history, job history before she registered that someone was talking to her. The information vanished behind data that kept refreshing and coming forward. The carpet she was sitting on was made by Italian fashion designer Antonio Bellagarda...

"...need help?" he said. "Miss? Miss?"

"Just dizzy," Sasha said, keeping her eyes closed. "Sorry, sorry." The faint rustle of his clothing as he moved closer to her instantly brought a picture from a catalogue in front of her eyes, a jumpsuit typical of a maintenance worker, complete with price and color swatches. The model turned and posed, showing the clothing from different angles. In another quadrant of her vision, the model's credits appeared, instantly being pushed to the background by information about all of the products that he had advertised and the different advertising agencies that were in charge of the various campaigns. She cracked her eyes open slightly and saw a dark haired man in front of her, definitely the man in the picture from her OverSight and definitely wearing a hotel worker's uniform, but according to the job history she had in her head, he was a professor from a local university, with...she frowned as she concentrated fiercely on filtering.

"I think we need to get you to a doctor," the man said. He seemed familiar somehow as well, beyond the fact that his entire citizen profile was somehow inside her head. Maybe he was from the seminar she was at earlier, but why would he be wearing coveralls?

She closed her eyes again, focusing on the man's voice without hearing what he was saying, letting it ground her as she breathed deeply. Her brain was beginning to handle the overload, passing it off to other systems that were usually redundant. Focusing on the man, seemed to have told her new library of information to begin digging deeper into the man's history, and a literal red flag appeared on the inside of her eyelids. She zoomed in on it, and read what was there. "Malcolm Sturm: Possible ties to a local anarchist group who have been suspected of several attempts to bring down OverSight headquarters and kill key employees."

The man seemed to have taken her lack of response as a

sign that she needed medical intervention even more than he had thought. She could feel his grip on her arm as he began to help her up and away from the support of the wall. Quickly, Sasha flipped through facial recognition (when had she gotten facial recognition? she wondered woozily) for recent matches and realized that he had been at the CyChip shop just after her, and before that she had seen his face on the citizen alert on the OverSight building, although he had been heavier in that photo and with blond hair. Here, his face was gaunt and there were more lines around his eyes. His citizen ID photo stayed superimposed on his real face until Sasha blinked and it vanished.

Faint glowing words still threatened to appear, especially around the edges of her vision, but she seemed to be able to control them better. Sasha could feel the knowledge potential, but she could manipulate it now, only feeling a mild pressure behind her eyes as if to let her know that she could let it loose at any time.

"Excuse me, Ms. Laren?" Sasha paused, suddenly realizing that she was halfway down the hall, going back toward the elevator with the man, Sturm. Casually, she tried to remove her arm from his by turning completely around to face the hotel uniformed man calling her. Smoothly, Sturm moved with her and his grip tightened slightly.

"Yes..." she paused as a full biography appeared. She quickly damped it down and just pulled his name up. "Tom?" She didn't think there had been a perceptible pause.

"Your seminar room is this way." He looked at the two of

them and frowned, apparently unsure why a guest would be arm in arm with what appeared to be a custodian. "Is there a problem?"

"No, no," Sturm said, cheerfully, letting go of her arm. "Just helping the lady. She wasn't feeling well." He backed up a little.

"You'd better get back to work," Tom said, voice cold at the apparent breach of propriety.

"I'd better get back to work," Sturm said, smiling, apparently without taking insult.

As the two men were talking, Sasha had opened a link to the OverSight emergency line. She took a 3D rendering of Malcolm Sturm, watching him as he spun around and went back toward the elevator, then hesitated and walked toward the stairwell behind a large tropical plant. After sending it, she glanced toward Tom, noticing his lips moving in a sub-vocal call, presumably to someone on his staff about the impolite behavior of one of the employees.

"If you will." Tom gestured toward the other end of the hallway where a set of large, polished wooden double doors stood, marking the entrance to the room where several hundred people were waiting on her. She took a deep breath, still somewhat wobbly, and walked through them.

Several hours later, Sasha was furious. It appeared that the faulty CyChip had not only wiped out all of her notes for her lecture, but it had overridden most of the data that she had stored in her system, including her call numbers for friends and colleagues and all of her personal financial packets and codes, leaving her without access to any bank or credit accounts. Fortunately, she knew most of the information for her lecture well enough that she could answer questions, otherwise she mostly allowed the other guests to carry the panel. She could tell that some of the more prominent scientists were somewhat disappointed in the lack of new information, but she didn't really care at this point. To top it all off, she could feel a deep ache beginning at the base of her spine around her OverSight hard drive, a sign of overuse that she hadn't experienced in years.

Leaving the lecture room, she went down to the lobby's OverSight repair and upgrade boutique in the hope that they would be able to recover some of her information. If all else failed, she could charge items to her account at the hotel, although the additional charges would drain her account rapidly. Before she could enter the store, an older man and a dark haired woman in blue grey OverSight uniforms stopped her.

"Sasha Laren?" the woman asked, showing a blank, silver badge. "I'm Janette Lee and this is my partner Sean Hiller. We understand that you saw a person of interest today and we'd like you to come with us so that we can take your statement."

Sasha rubbed the base of her neck. She hadn't bothered trying to see their badges. She was exhausted from holding off the fountains of information that surrounded her and she was starting to ache all over. "I have a few things that I need to take care of tonight. Is there any way that we could do this tomorrow?"

"I'm sure that a concerned citizen such as yourself would want to help OverSight in whatever ways are needed," Hiller said, putting away his own badge.

"Of course," Sasha said, sighing slightly. "Could I go to my room and get my jacket?"

Lee nodded, and the three went to the elevator. Arriving back at her room, Sasha waved her hand at the door, but the light remained stubbornly red and the door wouldn't open.

"I've been having some trouble with my OverSight today," Sasha began to explain.

"May I?" Hiller asked, pulling out his badge. Sasha nodded, and the man quickly overrode the door code, allowing them to enter.

"What?" Sasha's eyes widened as she saw the destruction of her room. Pillows had been slashed and shaken out, her suitcase had been emptied, the clothing scattered around the room. Lee and Hiller pushed her behind them, pulled out electro-pistols and covered the room, checking for anyone still there. When they pronounced the room clear, Sasha walked around trying to figure out if anything was missing.

"Don't touch anything," Lee warned, holstering her gun. "We've sent photos of the scene to OverSight but we'll still need to process it."

The two OverSight employees didn't speak during the short ride to the OverSight building, but Sasha could tell that they were in contact with each other from their movements. Sasha leaned back against the headrest of the computer controlled car and closed her eyes for a moment.

After the North American Civil War, many state and provincial governments had been crippled by the lack of available communication. With many satellites destroyed or in disrepair, OverSight had stepped in. Previously a purely entertainment corporation, the board of OverSight allowed their satellites and communications systems to be used by the governments. Maintaining a great deal of control, eventually OverSight had its own security and had slowly absorbed the previous governments until it was, in effect, the government. The takeover was a natural one, and OverSight had worked with many of the previous governments, providing them with closed circuit video feeds and other information. Sasha's parents had both been scientists employed by OverSight before they were killed in an attack on the company. Their work had given her the opportunity to have her pre-natal unit installed, and she had spent several years working for OverSight as well before branching off. She still maintained close ties and often visited lower security buildings to see old colleagues and as an official guest workshop coordinator, so she wasn't intimidated by the idea of going in.

Being with Lee and Hiller allowed her to bypass most of the security, only pausing briefly to be scanned for weapons. Her full neuro OverSight raised an eyebrow from the technician, but no comments. They made their way to a small hallway behind the main elevators where there was an unobtrusive door leading to an austere hallway. They arrived at a reinforced steel elevator which was waiting open for them.

Lee swiped the control panel with her badge and the doors shut with a muffled clang. The elevator descended and opened in a cement lined hallway lit with fluorescent lights several meters apart on the ceiling. The floor was also bare cement and their shoes echoed as they walked down the hall to one of the doors set firmly into the wall. Again, Lee waved her badge at the control panel and the three entered the room. The door shut silently behind them.

"Please sit down," Hiller said, gesturing toward the single chair on one side of the metal table. He sat down in one of the two chairs across from it while Lee stood, watching with her arms crossed. The chairs and table were all bolted to the floor, and Sasha realized that she was not just here as a witness.

"What's going on?" she asked, putting her hands on the table and leaning forward to Hiller.

"We'll be asking the questions, Ms. Laren," Lee said from the corner. The lights were shining on Sasha and she squinted to see the other woman in the shadows. "You're going to be here a while, so you might want to get comfortable."

Sasha sat down. She didn't like following orders, but she was exhausted, and it would be a useless piece of defiance to continue standing. "Well?"

"We understand that you had contact with known fugitive and insurgent Malcolm Sturm today," Hiller said.

"Yes, I sent you information about him when I realized who he was." Sasha rubbed her hand against the leg of her pants. "I recognized him and..."

"How did you recognize him?" Lee interrupted.

"His picture was on the OverSight screen this afternoon."

"Truth." There was no judgment in Lee's voice, just a statement of fact, probably retrieved from a vital signs packet designed to catch lies and omissions. "Had you seen him before you sent in the rendering of him?"

"Yes. I saw him in a shop, but didn't recognize him at the time."

"Truth. What was your interaction with him before the time you sent the rendering?"

"I...wasn't feeling well and he tried to help me."

"Evasion. What was your interaction with Malcolm Sturm before you sent the rendering?"

"That's the truth!" Sasha tried to stand and painfully bumped the back of her leg on the sturdy chair. She sat back down.

"Did Malcolm Sturm give you anything during either of the times that you saw him?"

"No."

"Truth. Did he transmit anything through your OverSight unit?"

"No."

"Evasion. What happened to your OverSight unit?"

"I don't know. It suddenly went haywire."

"Truth. When did it begin malfunctioning?"

"Just before I saw Sturm the second time, in the hotel." The room was warm and Sasha was perspiring.

"Truth." Lee's voice was thoughtful. "Did you do anything different with your OverSight before it started malfunctioning?"

"I had just bought a new CyChip, but it didn't work."

"Truth." The two officers conferred sub-vocally. "Was Malcolm Sturm at the shop where you purchased your CyChip?"

"Yes. I saw him as I was leaving."

"Truth." Lee walked forward and Sasha could see her more clearly as she entered the pool of light. "I think we have enough information for now. Make yourself comfortable. We'll be back shortly."

Before Sasha could react, Hiller stood and they left the room, the door closing behind them. With a cry, Sasha rushed to the door, discovering that it was locked. She pounded on it, succeeding only in hurting her hand.

Sasha must have slept because she was awakened by the door opening and someone entering. Momentarily forgetting about her malfunctioning OverSight, she called upon enhanced vision so that she could see better in the dimmed room. Lines and words spun around her sickeningly, but she was able to get them under control quickly and she focused on the person who had just entered the room.

Malcolm Sturm, age 37, Caucasian/Hispanic, read the display and she cut it off before it got further. It was all she needed to know. Getting ready to scream for help, she took a deep breath and began coughing as she inhaled something he sprayed toward her.

"I'm very sorry, but please don't worry," he said. "It's just something that will let us talk for a few minutes without you attracting attention to us. I won't harm you."

Sasha's throat cleared quickly, and she felt surprisingly good. Calm even, and she idly wondered what was in the spray. She looked down at some of the residue that had drifted onto the table and instantly the answer flashed beside it. *Ultrashort barbiturate, mild dose, central nervous system depressant, dosage will last approximately four minutes.* She nodded and turned to Malcolm, folding her hands in front of her.

"What do you want, Mr. Sturm?" she asked. Sturm looked surprised by her serenity, perhaps more than he was expecting, even with the drug.

He cleared his throat and looked embarrassed. "Well, I'm afraid we've had a little bit of a mix-up," he said. "It seems that you've accidentally picked up something that was intended for me."

"The CyChip I bought at the shop you were in this afternoon." Sasha's eyes unfocused slightly as she made the connections.

"Yes," he said. "It's a prototype of a new kind of OverSight, one that contains all the information about the OverSight corporation. It also has advanced facial recognition..."

"Advanced everything," Sasha said. "The information on it is very valuable."

"And very dangerous," Malcolm agreed. "Which is why we needed to intercept it."

"But I got to it first."

"Yes, and originally we thought that you were in the employ of OverSight, but it turns out that it was just a coincidence." Malcolm shrugged. "I realized that you had taken it unintentionally when I saw your reaction to the initialization. Someone was already searching your room at that point, but only found the blank CyChip."

"And then you tried to kidnap me in the hotel."

"No!" he protested. "I just wanted to extract the CyChip's information from your OverSight. You would have been perfectly safe."

"Well, you can't have it," Sasha said. "You're a terrorist group who deserves to be caught." A small countdown timer was ticking away at the bottom of her vision. Two minutes until the sedative wore off.

"It doesn't matter anyway," Malcolm said. "Because you have a fully integrated neural net, the OverSight can't be removed. It's been permanently embedded into your unit. If we remove it, your whole system will be wiped and you'll shut down."

"Well, then I suppose we've got a problem," Sasha said. Ninety seconds. "Because I won't go with you, and you've walked into the middle of a secure OverSight facility." She paused. "How did you get in here?"

"That doesn't matter," he said. "What matters is that I need you to come with me."

"Haven't you been listening?" she asked him, blinking. "I won't go with you. Your group killed my parents, many of my friends, and you want to shut down the corporation that keeps the peace across the entire continent. What is the percentage for me to come with you, especially since you'll be keeping me prisoner?"

"You're a prisoner here," he pointed out.

"I'm here as a witness."

"Witnesses aren't kept here. They're keeping you until they figure out your connection with me. Once they know that you have the only copy of the new OverSight, you'll definitely be staying here long term." He paused. "You won't be the only one. People who disagree with OverSight disappear. Sometimes their bodies are found."

"Wait, why isn't there another copy of it?" One minute.

"The only other copy was destroyed in an explosion several years ago and they haven't been able to reverse engineer it, as the scientists on the project disappeared at the same time."

"You mean they were killed." Like my parents, she thought.

"No," he said, exasperated. "I mean they disappeared. They went underground with us."

"So you're keeping them prisoner. How are you different from what you say OverSight is doing to me?" Thirty seconds.

"They came voluntarily because they knew that it was the right thing for them to do." He pulled a small silver disc out of his pocket and placed it on the table between them. "Just watch this and tell me what you think."

Sasha carefully turned her OverSight onto the small disc. A 3D hologram appeared in front of her. It was her parents, slightly older and dressed in unfamiliar clothing, which still evoked a science lab. "Mom? Dad?" Sasha's mouth parted in surprise.

"Sasha, this is a recording we've made so that Malcolm can convince you to come with him, to us," her father said. "We're so sorry that we had to disappear like that, but it was the only thing we could do to help people without putting you in danger."

"I thought you were dead," Sasha whispered.

"If there had been any other way, we wouldn't have left

you." Her mother was crying. "Listen to Malcolm, sweetie. There isn't much time."

"This is a trick," Sasha said, looking at Malcolm. He shook his head and gestured to the disc where the holograms were still talking.

"...don't believe us. But here goes. Your first word was cat. Your favorite color is purple and you had a stuffed, white cat you called Sassy."

"You wet your bed when you were fifteen, and made me promise never to tell anyone."

Her father turned to her mother in genuine surprise. "She did?" he asked, and Sasha could hear laughter from off screen, presumably the person operating the 3D camera.

"I'm sorry, baby, but it was something that you would know that was completely secret," her mother said. "Please, come and yell at me in person. I love you." The disc blinked back to silver.

Sasha was torn by joy, rage and humiliation. "I'm going to kill her," she breathed as she picked up the disc.

"Does that mean you'll come with me?" Malcolm asked.

The sedative had worn off, and it was difficult to focus the OverSight again. "I think you'd better get me another dose of that stuff. It helps bring down my nervous system activity and I can concentrate better."

Malcolm handed her the spray bottle, just as alarms sounded and lights started flashing. Sasha inhaled a quick breath of it and tucked it into her pocket beside the disc.

"Looks like we're going to have company," Malcolm said.

"Time to move." He pulled out a security card and flashed it in front of the access panel. Nothing happened.

"Let me try," Sasha said, holding out her hand for the card. "If this OverSight has all of the corporation's information, maybe I can override their security." She looked at the card and a schematic of lines and dots appeared, twisted and settled down in a new pattern. She tried passing it in front of the access panel and the door opened.

"Well." Malcolm said, looking dumbfounded. "I had thought I would be rescuing you, but it doesn't look like you need it."

They left the room, closing the door behind them and Sasha brought up the schematics of the building they were in, including camera angles and security patterns. They easily avoided most of the employees of OverSight, except for a few that Malcolm needed to stun with an electro-pistol. They quickly made their way up to the surface via an old service tunnel that emerged several blocks from the OverSight building and walked away.

The Cageless Zoo

written by

Thomas K. Carpenter

ABOUT THE AUTHOR
Thomas K. Carpenter resides near St. Louis with his wife Rachel and their two children. He earned his degree in Metallurgical Engineering from the University of Missouri Rolla. After finishing up his M.B.A. in the summer of 2006, he returned to his roots of writing fiction. When he's not busy writing his next book, he's playing soccer in the yard with his kids or getting beat by his wife at cards. He keeps a regular blog at www.thomaskcarpenter.com.

The Cageless Zoo

SEE THE GALAXY'S ONLY CAGELESS ZOO

The glittery sign hung above the rows of vehicles. Melandre gripped Natalya's slender shoulder and held her tight as a tour bus rumbled past.

GRAB THE LION'S TAIL

Letters scrolled across the hazy morning, right above the weather beaten green-copper domes, scattered across the grounds like giant moss-covered rocks. When they neared the zoo, Andrake had said it looked like a bunch of tortoises waiting to eat the people strolling through the entrance. His sister, Natalya, had told him that tortoises were vegetarian and then they'd argued until Melandre, with hushed intensity, told them to be quiet.

SHAKE HANDS WITH THE CHTHULU-BEAST

Andrake, her eleven-year old son, hung back, fiddling with a hacking wand.

"That's the ambreimareus," her daughter said, indicating the sign with her free hand. "And it has tentacles, not hands."

"Hmm..." Melandre acknowledged the comment, then spun back, yelling at Andrake. "Quit dawdling!"

She accessed her son's system and sent a flash of light across his eye-screens.

"Didn't have to do that, mum," said Andrake as he shoved the hacking wand in his pocket and rubbed his eyes. "I was almost done."

MEET THE GALAXY'S MOST DEADLY PREDATORS ALL IN ONE ZOO

He gave his mother a crooked you're-always-hassling-me smirk and an eye roll.

Melandre's heart dropped a few inches. He looked just like his father when he did that and then before she could close that door in her mind she recalled the last time she saw Philippe—walking out the door with a knapsack slung over his shoulder, scruffy black hair barely hiding his gray eyes, smiling and winking as he slid into the Darwin Institute vehicle. He promised he'd be back in three months.

Since his death, she hadn't been sure she could raise their two children alone. They were still so young.

"Who's dawdling now, mum?" Andrake tugged at her shirt.

Natalya gave her hand a squeeze. "You need to do this. We all do." Her daughter's eyes moistened at the corners. Melandre felt her own well up.

"Plus, it'll be fun!" And like that, the rainstorm was gone. At least for her daughter.

Natalya ran ahead through the entrance, coffee-skin soaking up the light of the morning sun. Andrake chased his sister and they tumbled into the park, laughing and even holding hands.

Melandre checked the horizon back toward Steelzine. Faint ochre-colored clouds perched above the city. Sand storm coming. Still an hour before it would overtake the zoo.

Around the corner under the first dome, she found Natalya petting a lion laying in the shade of a great arching tree, tail undulating in the manufactured breeze. A few onlookers stood near: Tansies, Church-folk, Hyllers, Earthlings like herself, and the like. Not as many as she thought might visit. Varagen was still a new planet in the Federation.

The way the lion stared peacefully in the distance while her daughter stroked its creamy fur unnerved her. She knew the eye-screens painted an augmented reality overtop to hide them behind. Made them appear as another lion on the savannah or not at all, depending on the program's logic matrix.

But still, adrenaline shot through her veins, making her breath quicken. It's unnatural to mingle with the beasts, she thought. They used to hunt us. And technology doesn't always protect us, nor did it protect my husband. That's when she saw the sign, as if it were waiting for her to remember.

SEE THE FEARSOME HYWAKALAR—THE FLOWER-TOOTHED LIZARD

A full-sized representation painted across her own eye-screens—an advertisement featuring one of the zoo's assorted creatures. Its horrid green body was low to the ground like a speedster. Long protruded nose sported a split-row of teeth that opened like some toothy flower, both horizontally and vertically. The beastie roared and she swore it mocked her.

Turning her back on the phantom Hywakalar, she sensed Andrake causing trouble. She crept around a grove of trees to find him hiding between two colorful booths that printed up trinkets on demand, pointing his hacking wand at an acarnocrat in his thick, layered metallic garments. The man swatted at a giant ghost moth buzzing around his head as her son silently laughed at him from his hiding spot.

Melandre grabbed him by the ear. "Turn it off."

"Ow!" When the acarnocrat stopped flailing, she took the tube and shoved it into her pocket. "You can have it back when we leave."

"I'm just having fun." Andrake spread his hand passively and his boyish smile again reminded her of his father.

Melandre collected her daughter and pulled up the map that downloaded to their systems when they'd arrived. A floating representation of interconnected domes hovered between them and when they tapped the domes, floating animals appeared. They could touch the animals and learn more about them, but they didn't bother. Natalya had memorized facts about them all and had lectured them on the various abilities of the zoo's predators while they rode from Steelzine.

They agreed to see thirty animals, about a quarter of the park. It's all Melandre thought she could handle. The Institute man could catch up when he arrived.

Before they continued, Melandre found a guard in a blue checkered shirt that seemed both authoritarian and comical. His eyes blinked twice, slowly, as if he viewed her through a fog.

"What happens if they get loose?" she asked.

He blinked once again. "They are loose."

"No." She felt foolish all at once for asking her question. "What if they attack someone? The animals?"

"They won't."

"But what if they do?" Her children pulled at her arm, but their embarrassment hardened her resolve.

The guard sighed. "The central computer monitors all the guests. If any beast makes a move, it shocks them. Or if that doesn't work, we can shock them. We have the codes."

She glanced around. "You're the only guard I've seen."

He shrugged. "Were more of us when the park opened. But seeing nothing has happened, they let some of us go each year."

"Try to have some fun, mum," she heard Natalya say. When the slender fingers, smaller, but yet similar to her own, entangled themselves, the tension that'd been building in her loosened slightly.

"Okay," she said thinking that her daughter was right. She'd be a fool to think something would happen today. Or any day for that matter. It's just that her husband had told her that nothing would happen on his last expedition, too.

She clapped her hands, trying to dispel any doubts about coming to the cageless zoo.

"Which first—the crystalline creeper or the great white shark? They're both close." Melandre gave her children an honest smile, at least to the point that she'd try to have fun.

"Oh, mum." Andrake pushed his hand through his dark

hair. "I programmed a route for us while you talked to the guard. Using that Catcher's Dilemma algorithm you showed me last week optimizing against current crowd density and minimizing distance traveled."

She tussled his hair as he hooked his hand on the corner of her pocket. "I'm certain the Mechatronics Guild will be pleased when you sign up."

They wandered the domes, her kids running ahead to interact with the animals. Natalya had thought the darvi had been the cutest. An adjective Melandre couldn't quite manage to conjure for the scaly swamp-hunter with jagged teeth, but she *was* her father's daughter. She'd been bringing home nasty little oozes and stick bugs to care for as long as Melandre could remember.

Melandre preferred the sterile computers and mechatronics that performed exactly as expected. But she did enjoy the enthusiasm that her husband Philippe and now Natalya had for the animal kingdom, as unreliable as the creatures were.

After a dozen domes, the kids' excitement unwavering, they neared the backend of the zoo. Raspy wails from the sandstorm outside muted the swamp noises from the dome they'd just exited.

"Good morning, Mrs. Calderon." The voice startled her and erased the good feeling she been enjoying.

"Mr. Hisler." She shook his hand, remembering meeting him once with Philippe at a company gathering. His wispy black hair, sagging jowls and grayish skin reminder her then, and now, of a half-burnt candle.

Her kids ran ahead to the next dome, passing through the wide hallways that connected them. They went to see the tempest, a creature from Giant's Belt that looked like the mythical dragon.

"I'm pleased you were able to come, Mrs. Calderon." He paused and licked his lips. "May I call you Melandre? You can call me, Raul."

"Mrs. Calderon will do, Mr. Hisler." She kept her hands clasped in front. As she brushed her leg, she realized that Andrake's hacking wand was missing. Then she remembered him sidling next to her. If she didn't have the Institute man to deal with she'd march ahead and give her son a lesson.

A group of chattering Tansies in their flowery garb passed them. Raul Hisler waited until they were gone before speaking again. But as he opened his mouth, the wailing of the sandstorm blasting the zoo increased its volume.

"I bet the sandstorm makes maintaining the zoo quite expensive," Melandre said, looking upward.

"Certainly," Raul replied. "Last year we had a wall collapse in one of the domes. The sandstorm lasted three days and kept us from repairing it. Thankfully the vegetation in the dome was quite resilient and grew back quickly after the event."

"That's lucky," Melandre mumbled.

After a long pause Raul spoke again. "We at the Darwin Institute are quite pleased that you've agreed to turn over your husband's research files." Raul parted his thin lips to reveal faded yellow teeth.

"I haven't agreed to turn over anything," she said, more

sharply than she had intended.

She held back her desire to apologize, deciding that he didn't deserve it.

"By the agreements your husband signed, in return for funding for his research, all information was property of the Institute."

Melandre flared her nostrils. "I don't care about those agreements. These are his private journal files."

"The agreements state that all information recorded during the length of the term, no matter what the location of the data, would be property of the Institute."

His tone reminded her of a lawyer. She paused under the archway, putting a hand on her hip.

"So you're going to tell me that if he sent me a love letter, *that* would be owned by you creeps?"

He nodded almost apologetically. "Technically speaking, yes. But we're only really interested in the epigenetic research. We'd probably delete any love letters."

Melandre knew that Raul's words were true. She'd read the agreements herself, but she had hoped they wouldn't try to enforce all of them. Philippe had been so desperate for funding, he'd signed away all his rights.

"But the Institute will bury his research. It'll never see the light of day." She threw her hands in the air. "They only funded him so they could control the results."

Raul cleared his throat. "The Darwin Institute is a prestigious establishment with centuries of history. They would never *bury* research. Especially expensively funded research."

"Please don't patronize me with your company bullshit, Mr. Hisler." The anger rose up unexpected. "Philippe had been blocked on numerous occasions when he tried to publish his work. The Darwin family hegemony, who still controls a majority of the Institute, has some long standing feud with a dead Frenchman named Lamarck."

Raul peeled his lips back in a sneer. "Lamarck was a hack and a fraud that tried to promote that animals could change form from one generation to the next based on their environment. Even a school taught child knows that a giraffe's neck doesn't get longer because it *needs* to eat the higher levels. Only natural selection can do that and only over multiple generations."

Raul placed his hands behind his back, raised his chin and looked down his flattened nose. "So when your dear departed husband tried to regurgitate the works of this fraudster who's been discredited for centuries, he wasn't blocked because of a feud. He was blocked because he was wrong and the research didn't support it."

Melandre slapped him, hard. Raul put his hand to his jaw and continued speaking. "So you can thank the Institute's generosity that it funded him at all and that it kept his inadequacies as a scientist from the general public."

She thought about slapping him again, but decided she'd gone far enough. She was afraid the kids might have seen her loss of control. Her moods brewed vicious storms these days when she least expected it.

The kids appeared from the tunnel, laughing, but came up short when they saw their mother's face.

"Everything's fine," she said. "Let's go to the next exhibit."

Raul gave her children his pasty smile. "Your mother was just explaining she would be handing over your father's research so it can receive a treasured place in our revered Institute."

Natalya raised an eyebrow. "I thought you Darwin originalists hated my father's work? Couldn't understand how it added to Darwin's legacy, not reduced it."

"Well, little girl. How old are you?" Raul asked in a condescending tone.

"Thirteen." Natalya stared back undaunted.

"Well, thirteen year-old girls can't understand the complexities of biological research nor the scientific rigors of publication." Raul smirked.

Natalya spoke next in an airy sing-song voice. "Biological complexities?" Then she scrunched her face at the Institute man.

Melandre had to contain a laugh. She could see the fierce look in her daughter's eyes and knew the man was in trouble.

Natalya put her hands behind her back, mimicking the same practiced pose that Raul had.

"I guess it would be too difficult for 'a little girl' to understand how environmental stressors can create biological responses turning on and off the methyls that make up the epigenome, emphasizing one gene or the other and allowing traits to change from one generation to the next without changing DNA. And the epigenome — which is something of a misnomer of a term since it's made up of a couple of systems that all regulate the effect of DNA in an individual — can be sensitive to any number of environmental effects like changing prey or predators, or temperatures, or anything really, if nature designs it so."

Natalya finished by sticking her tongue out at Raul, who looked more stunned than she thought possible. Melandre's heart almost exploded from pride. Her daughter had done with words what she couldn't do with a slap.

Raul regained his composure. "All your posturing doesn't change the fact that the Institute owns the data. Like it or not, you must hand over the data or face legal challenges."

Melandre held back her anger and decided to plead. "Do you not have any compassion that my husband gave his life for his research?" She noticed the dome they had come to and pointed to the sign at the edge of the jungle within. As if on cue, a hywakalith tramped out of the undergrowth of purple leaves and spiky fronds, and roared.

"That's the very species that killed him—the flower-toothed lizard." Her skin crawled as she watched it stroll back into the jungle. She decided then she wasn't going into the next dome.

Raul stared at her, his eyes dead to her pleading, raising his voice above the noise of the sandstorm outside. "This is the type of nonsense your husband wanted to spread. It was the hywlarkana, the lightning lizard, a cousin to the hywakalith that killed him, though no one knows how that species came that far north out of its range."

"It didn't roam from its territory," Melandre said. "Philippe induced the environmental stressors from the southern badlands to affect the hywakalith so it would give birth to the hywlarkana.

It's not a different species, it keeps a variety of tools in its DNA and emphasizes one or the other depending on its location. The jungle can't support its static blast due to the humidity so it represses that gene." Melandre sighed. "If they'd actually captured one they could have proved it, but the one that killed him disappeared and the ones from the badlands have only been seen by the locals very rarely."

"All your arguments are pointless." Raul sighed and rubbed his temple. "If I don't collect the data today, they'll just send someone else later. And while I don't agree with Philippe's continuation of Lamarck's research, he did find and catalog many unknown species for the Institute and he is remembered fondly by the other researchers."

He was clearly trying to make amends for his earlier comments, though it irked her that Philippe hadn't been remembered fondly by Raul. Melandre didn't know why she was arguing with him, except that she needed to blame someone for her husband's death. She realized she had her arms crossed and that her children were watching her. If they were going to do well without a father, she had to make sure they understood when battles were unwinnable and to move on.

"Fine...," she paused, closing her eyes and feeling like she was making a mistake. "Philippe's data is contained within this." She held out her hand and a rotating puzzle cube formed, representing all of his journal files.

Raul touched the cube and it faded slowly as the data transferred. Melandre sensed Andrake's mischief, but when she turned her head to see what he was doing, he had his hands behind his back.

When the cube disappeared, Raul opened his mouth briefly, then after a pause, closed it and walked down the tunnel toward the jungle dome leaving Melandre alone with her children.

She felt tears welling up and bit on her lip to stop them. Andrake and Natalya circled her in their arms and squeezed. She thought it should be her comforting them.

"Do you want to leave, mum?" Natalya asked.

"Uh huh," she mumbled, nodding her head. "We can come back another time if you want. The zoo wasn't as bad as I thought it'd be."

"It's been fantastic," Natalya said, spinning on her heels. Andrake nodded enthusiastically.

"Can we see the cthulhu-beast before we go? I wanted to give it a hug but the Tansies were hogging him, recording immersives and being so slow about it," Natalya said.

Melandre smiled at her children. "Sure. It's right here after all. And then we can go."

Moist, rotten air assaulted them as they left the tunnel passage and entered the swamp dome. A vending machine printed rubber boots to wear after scanning their feet. They were about to enter the marsh when the power flickered twice and then went out.

"Oh shit," Melandre whispered under her breath as the emergency lights glowed on.

"Mum, was that supposed to happen?" Andrake asked, adjusting his pant leg stuck into his boot.

"No way, you big dummy," Natalya told her brother.

That's when they heard the screaming. Melandre backed her children toward the tunnel entrance. The screaming wasn't the just a frightened yell, but the sound of great pain.

"Oh god." It was all Melandre could think to say.

"That group of Tansies was probably still posing with the cthulhu-beast when the power went out," Natalya whimpered. "When the eye-screens stopped working..."

Suddenly, a commotion erupted in the swamp. A shape moved in the darkness toward them. In the dim light, they could see the colorful garb of a Tansie. Melandre reflexively reached out her hand toward the man running through the slimy hanging vines, water splashing as he had to lift his knees high. He was almost out.

Then the swamp reached out and swallowed him. Melandre got the impression of tentacles flowing out of the darkness and dragging the man back. At least he didn't scream.

Melandre closed her eyes for a moment, gathering her strength. She really wished Philippe was here, but since he wasn't she would have to do all she could.

She gathered her children to her. "We're going to go a different way. Keep near me and we can get through this."

Natalya glanced around frantically. "Can't we stay right here? Until someone comes and gets us?"

"No, sweetie," she said. "We're going to have to get out ourselves. With the sandstorm, no one can get here and you heard the guard. There aren't many of them."

"Can we go outside?" Andrake asked.

She shook her head. "The sandstorm would suffocate us

and strip our skin down to the bones."

Then they heard yelling from the other direction, toward the hywakalith dome. She recognized the voice immediately. It was a scared yelling and not a pained scream.

"Come with me, quietly."

They crept down the tunnel until they could see the tall fronds illuminated by the emergency lights. They stayed to the edge, glancing behind them occasionally toward the swamp. They hadn't heard any more screams from back that way.

At the threshold of the jungle dome, they could hear Raul screaming, "Help me!"

The Institute man was up in a tree while a hywakalith prowled beneath him, splitting its nasty grin and showing its four rows of teeth.

Raul saw them at the entrance and started waving, nearly falling out of the tree. "Help me, please! I don't want to die!" Melandre could hear the sobbing in his voice.

Melandre checked around for a weapon, but the only object in sight was a trash bin against the wall. She couldn't believe she was trying to save him, after what he'd just done to her. But he was her species, kind of.

She thought about getting the trashcan to throw at the beast, but then it would just turn on her and she had no way to defend herself. She was about to go back to the other dome to find something when Andrake pushed his way in front of her.

When he pulled the hacker wand from his pocket she wanted to cuff his ear. Now was not the time for punishment though. Her son pointed the wand at the hywakalith and a ghost moth appeared by its head. It took until the moth practically flew down its throat before the beast noticed it. Then it checked back up with Raul and probably deciding the food in the tree was too far away, snapped at the moth. When the moth flew away, the hywakalith chased it until it disappeared into the jungle.

Raul jumped down from the tree and upon impact, rolled onto his back, holding his ankle. He was making too much noise as he groaned.

"Stay here," she whispered and ran to Raul, helping him to his feet. Her back felt exposed as she helped him limp back to the tunnel.

"Thank you," he said too loud and both kids shushed him.

They moved to a point between the two domes and huddled around. Melandre eyed Raul's ankle with worry. He would slow them down if they had to run.

"Through the cthulhu-beasts or the hywakaliths?" she asked. "We have to go through one dome or the other."

Raul's eyes wavered. Melandre snapped her fingers in front of his eyes. "Raul, stay with us. I need another adult here."

He shook his head as if just waking up and nodded drunkenly.

Natalya took a big breath. "I think we should go through the swamp." She bit her lip. "The cthulhu-beasts have a huge appetite, but there were twelve Tansies and if I remember correctly, only two creatures in the swamp. Six people each should be enough to sate them."

Natalya shrugged her shoulders.

"Good thinking, sweetie," she said, glad to have a reason

not to go back to the jungle dome. She didn't want to lose her whole family to the same beast. "We'll skirt the edge of the dome. Maybe we won't even see either one of them."

"I don't understand," Raul said, speaking to himself. "They have backup generators if the power goes out. And why haven't the guards shocked the animals?"

"I don't know," said Melandre.

"It has to be sabotage or something. That many systems couldn't fail at once," he said. "At least we'll be able to say it wasn't the Institute's fault."

Melandre speared him in her sights. "Whose fault doesn't matter right now. People have already died. Don't worry about your precious Institute's reputation. Let's worry about keeping my children alive."

A scream erupting from the tunnel behind snapped Raul out of his stupor. He nodded and motioned Melandre to lead on as they hobbled together.

Raul didn't have boots and their combined weight sunk them into the mud along the wall, so their progress was slow. They all kept their gaze trained on the swamp expecting an attack at any time. The spaces between the emergency lights were far enough that they traveled through darkness between. Melandre expected to feel a slimy tentacle grab her leg each time.

Near the end, they found a section of ripped colorful garb hanging on the end of a twisted tree branch. They all stopped and stared solemnly before Melandre motioned them to keep moving.

When they reached the other end and crossed into the connecting tunnel, Melandre felt a load lift from her shoulders, even before she pushed Raul away to rest. Maybe they would make it.

"Which way now?" she asked. The tunnel led away in two other directions besides the one they came from.

"The power station is near the exit," Raul said. "But frankly, if we make it that far, I'm getting the hell out of here."

"I think we've got a lot more to worry about before the exit. We were on the far side of the zoo."

"The tempest lies down that tunnel and a pack of hyenas down that way." Natalya pointed to the right-most direction.

Raul snorted. "God, that awful tempest. I argued against placing that stupid creature here. They only included it since it reminded people of dragons."

"I thought it was beautiful," said Natalya. "But you are right about their dangerousness. They're only deadly when they have heavy winds to catch their sails on. Otherwise, they're really slow."

"Sounds like we have a winner," said Melandre.

They started to move that direction when Andrake spoke up. "Wait. Maybe we shouldn't go that way."

They all stared at him until he explained. "That creature may be easy to get past, but what about the other ones beyond? Shouldn't we figure the total route?"

Melandre grabbed her son and gave him a big hug. "Good thinking, scamp."

She looked to Natalya. "What's after the tempest?"

It took them longer than she liked and she felt vulnerable the whole time discussing the pros and cons of each animal that they would have to get past to escape. Raul had a lot of valuable information to add, though she thought her daughter had the more insightful conclusions like the one about the cthulhu-beast. As horrible as it was, her choice in direction had probably saved their lives. In the end, they chose the route past the tempest.

The dome was a grassy plain with strange fungal trees. They kept to the edge and along the way, snapped off a crutch for Raul from a spindly tree with tufts of fronds on the ends of each branch.

The flatness of the landscape afforded them a good sight line so they crossed it without worry of its predator. The tempest had escaped to other parts of the zoo.

Following their preplanned route, they took the left passage of the three-way. Melandre had argued against this dome, due to its unique challenges, but the other way took them past the highly territorial mountain gorillas. Both Natalya and Raul had agreed that the gorillas would pose the greater challenge.

The next dome was different than the previous ones they had visited. Instead of a half-sphere, the bottom had been carved out and it was a full sphere with multiple spindly bridges stretching across the gap. On either side, cliff walls rose up from below with bushes sticking out of crevices and cracks. This was the largest dome in the cageless zoo, twice the size of any other.

Five paths snaked across: one along each cliff wall and three across the middle, lined with emergency lights. The tallest arched through the center. The two along the side climbed up until they neared the nests of the great deathtalon hawks with wide platforms for large groups to observe. They were named because of the brain liquefying poison contained within their claws. One scratch would kill within a few hours.

Natalya pointed at the upper reaches of the cliffs. "The zoo has four deathtalons. One mated pair with a chick on the right cliff and a lone female on the left. The other mate died last year to a mysterious disease."

"I think it's the mated pair on the left," Raul countered.

"No. I'm certain it's the other way."

"Um." Andrake, standing at the edge of the railing, pointed down to the bottom of the dome. "Do we really have to pass this one?"

The others moved to the edge. Six bodies lay scattered across the rocks including two children.

Natalya cleared her throat. "The deathtalon is known to be a cruel killer. Dropping its prey from great heights when it's full."

"I wonder how many they've eaten so far?" Andrake asked.

"It's worse than that," Raul said. "When they scratch you, the first part of your brain to go is your muscle control. Their catch usually get fed to the babies alive while they can still feel it."

"I think that factoid doesn't help us one bit, Mr. Hisler," Melandre growled between clenched teeth.

Raul looked to the two kids and then back to Melandre. He mouthed the word *sorry*.

"Does anyone see a bird?" Melandre asked to distract them.

Andrake spied one bird perched on a tree growing out from the cliff along the left wall. The others were not to be seen.

"Which path?" Melandre asked.

After a long silence, Natalya spoke up. "The path along the right wall will keep us out of that lone female's territory. I'm guessing we haven't seen the other two because they're feeding."

Melandre could tell from her daughter's hunched shoulders she was unsure about her conclusions. Raul only shrugged when she checked with him.

"Right it is."

Before they stepped onto the ramp, she grabbed the lid to the trashcan.

"Good idea, mum." Natalya said. "I'll go get the one back from the other dome."

Her daughter ran back the other way before she could stop her. Melandre's heart labored in her chest the whole time she was gone. The relief was palpable when she returned.

"Use your ghost moth if you think it might help," she said to Andrake. He saluted her with his hacking wand.

"Wait?" Raul said. "That made the ghost moth?"

"Yeah. Beams the images through your security system to make you see a moth," Andrake said proudly. "I finished making it last week."

"Got anything else in there?"

"No." Andrake shook his head.

Melandre could see Raul's mind working. "What are you thinking?"

"Well, the zoo works by projecting an augmented reality

into the animal's systems. Keeping track of the world and hiding the guests."

"Prey, you mean," Natalya said.

"Not now," said Melandre.

Raul nodded. "It's okay. Prey is right. But they carry a power system with them just like we do. If we can get the codes, we can push into their systems and shock them with that wand."

"It doesn't have much range," Andrake explained. "Back at the hywakalith dome, that was about as far as it reaches."

"Well that doesn't help us right now," Melandre said. "But if we find a guard, we'll be sure to do that. Let's get moving before the birds get hungry again."

The four headed out onto the right ramp, Melandre and Natalya in front with trash can lids held in front of them like shields, Andrake with his hacking wand and Raul limping behind last with his make-shift cane.

The deathtalon on the other side of the dome shrieked at them as they traveled across, but it stayed on its perch. As they neared the platform with the nest, Melandre noticed her daughter's trash can lid shaking. Natalya's lower lip was trembling, but she had scrunched her eyes like when she had lectured Raul. Melandre flashed her a reassuring smile, though it felt forced. She was terrified herself.

As they neared the edge of the platform, one of the deathtalons released a bone-shaking screech. Natalya dropped her lid and it rattled across the ground. Melandre pulled her daughter down and the others followed. They hid on the slope of the ramp. She could hear her daughter's heartbeat even above her own.

Melandre grabbed the lid with her sweaty fingers, handing it to Natalya and motioned for them to continue. The two deathtalons rested in their huge nest, preening themselves. They were bigger than Melandre thought they'd be. She imagined their wingspans to be at least twenty feet. Chirping from a chick could be heard from the nest, though they couldn't see it.

Creeping at the farthest point from the nest, they shuffled around the platform. A couple of boulders blocked them from view until they were about halfway across. Then the shortest section of the nest wall revealed its contents. Andrake gasped and Natalya whimpered when they looked.

Inside the nest, two men and one woman were set against the side like manikins. The taller man was clearly dead with his arm bitten off and dark viscous blood congealed along the rocks. But the other two were clearly alive. Their wide eyes followed them as they moved past.

There was nothing they could do for them. Even if the birds weren't guarding them, they'd be dead in a few hours. But that didn't make her feel any better about leaving them.

Raul must have been concentrating on his walking because he didn't acknowledge the horrible sight in the nest until they were nearly to the end of the platform. Then he exclaimed much too loudly, "God have mercy." And dropped his crutch.

The clatter of the wood against the platform resulted in two soul rending shrieks from the nest. The two deathtalons spread their wings defensively.

"Run!" Melandre yelled.

A deathtalon tore across the platform and Melandre barely got her lid up in time to deflect a claw. Her children had already started down the ramp. Helping Raul limp across she eyed the second bird that stayed in its nest, protecting the chick with its wings stretched wide. She knew the other bird was circling around.

Andrake and Natalya tore down the ramp ahead of her while she urged Raul on faster. Torn between helping the injured man and protecting her children, she found herself about halfway between them when the deathtalon made its attack.

The bird swooped down onto Andrake. Its deadly claws outstretched in front to snatch her child from the ramp. She was too far to do anything. She was certain that nothing could be done, when Natalya ran back up the ramp and launched her trash can lid at the bird. It spun through the air and hit the bird's body enough to make it veer slightly. Andrake dove at that moment and the bird's talons missed him by a hair.

Its huge wingspan meant it would have to make another long circuit before attacking again. She screamed for them to keep running. They might make it with only one more attack.

When her children reached the bottom, she felt relief. At least until she checked to her left to find the deathtalon streaming toward her. Then in the space between, a ghost moth appeared and the bird stopped its descent and tried to attack the insect. This gave her and Raul enough time to make it down the ramp to safety.

They scooted down the hall away from the railing in case the birds could slip through the tunnel. When it landed on the railing and screeched at them, they knew they were safe.

Bent over and heaving, they caught their breath. With the adrenaline of their flight slipping away, Melandre's shoulder throbbed. She checked the lid to find a deep gouge in the metal. After a few minutes rest, so her legs could stop shaking, they left the tunnels.

Moving to the next dome, inhabited by a pack of sand devils in an arid desert, they found a half-eaten man in a blue and white checkered shirt at the entrance. Melandre put her hand to her mouth. The kids shared glances while Raul refused to meet her eyes.

"Fine," she said and inched up to the body as the heat from the dome brought a bead of sweat to her forehead. Melandre held her breath and used the remainder of the dead man's shirt to hide his face. Somehow it was easier to look at him when he wasn't vacantly staring back. Raul and her kids came up after she was done.

"Can you get the codes?" Raul asked, poking the dead man with his crutch.

Andrake pointed his hacking wand and shook his head. "No computer. Whatever ate him ate the computer."

"If the sand devils did it, then we're out of luck." Raul said staring out into the desert dome. "They drag their prey into tunnels and eat them down there."

Natalya crouched next to the man, holding her nose and looking at the wounds. "It wasn't the sand devils that killed him. They have small mouths. Whatever killed this guard had a big bite."

Her thoughtful pose and investigative eye reminded her of Philippe.

"Good job, sweetie," Melandre said.

"Well that doesn't help us unless we can find the beastie," Raul said.

Melandre noticed marks in the sand. "Looks like tracks over here."

They crowded around the trail, careful not to damage the evidence. Natalya indicated two separate prints with her fingers. "I think whatever was eating this man got chased into the dome by another one."

"Here's a good print." Andrake waved them over.

"That's a lion," Natalya said right away.

"Yep," said Raul. "You're going to be quite the biologist like your father."

Even though he had insulted them earlier, it was quite a compliment from an Institute man. Natalya beamed with pride and for a brief moment, Melandre forgot they were trying to escape with their lives.

"I can't tell what the other print is," said Natalya.

Raul shrugged after a brief examination.

"Let's follow them," Melandre suggested. "Hopefully they've injured each other enough that we can get the computer back."

"I don't even need it physically," said Andrake. "Just close enough to connect."

They followed the tracks while scouting for other predators. The desert dome had a slight rise to it so they couldn't see across the sand.

The tracks led to a small incline and they found one of the predators, a huge grotesque shambler with green blood leaking from its wounds. The area around the dead shambler was rife with gouges and scrapes.

"Computer's not here," said Andrake, pointing his wand at the dead creature. Long slimy filaments hung in a blanket around it.

Raul pointed to the center of the dome. "I think the sand devils got the lion."

In the distance on a far rise, four blackish red shapes dragged another whitish one along the ridge.

Melandre pushed Raul lightly in the direction of the sand devils. "If we hurry we can get the codes before they pull it underground."

They moved out across the sand with Andrake holding his wand in front like he was divining for water. But not long after, the sand devils disappeared into the ground.

"Almost had it," Andrake said shaking his head.

As they neared, they could see a concrete path leading into a depression in the sand. Cautiously, they followed the path. Melandre clutched the trash can lid until her fingers whitened at the knuckles.

They met no resistance and followed the trail into the ground. The right wall transformed into a clear barrier with tunnels on the other side. Passages with see-through walls lead in further.

"The sand devil tunnels are unstable so we had to make safe

ones," Raul whispered.

"Yes, clearly you were thinking of safety when you designed this death trap," said Melandre.

"Not now." Natalya squeezed her arm and both the adults nodded their truce.

Andrake motioned toward the center tunnel. Melandre hoped the sand devils kept to their part of the tunnel complex. As the ground swallowed them up, she grabbed Natalya's hand. Being underground caused her hand to tremble. Her daughter flashed her a reassuring smile.

The signal led them deeper in until they rounded a corner and found two sand-devils fighting over an object the size of a leg. At first Melandre thought the sand devils were in the same passage as they were, but then she realized they were protected by the see-through wall. The black and red striped creatures reminded her of a cross between an ant and a feral dog. They had six legs with the front pair sporting pincers. Milky white eyes lolled in their heads.

Two sand devils tore at a piece of meat, mauling it with their wide mouths. Gray foam dripped from their lips. They could see movement in dark tunnels beyond the two sand devils.

After watching for a moment, Andrake led them further in. They found the lion around the next bend being feasted on by three sand devils. Her gaze fixed on the grotesque spectacle until her son gave them the thumbs up after a few minutes silently accessing his personal interface.

"Test it," she whispered.

Andrake nodded and then held the hacking wand in front

of him. Melandre didn't think it was going to work at first when they kept gnawing on the corpse. Then the three sand devils shuddered and fell on their sides convulsing.

Andrake kept it there until she told him, "That's enough."

They wound back through the tunnels and reached the arid sand without incident. The sand devils had collected enough prey that they weren't active at the moment. Melandre hoped it was only other predators that they had found.

Using the guard codes to shock the predators they were able to by-pass the next seven domes without incident. Three of the domes had been empty, their predators wandered off or eaten by another. Of the four with creatures—a darkaron, a pair of hyllion wolves, a pack of cygerons and a huge horned gorenaut; a few shocks from the wand and they ran off.

As they neared the entrance dome, Melandre tried to steel herself from feeling any relief. They weren't out yet, though she wanted to grab her children and run. It saddened her they hadn't found any other survivors along the way. When the predators had been let loose, they must have turned on the people immediately. They would have met the same fate had they not been in the tunnel and used the tricks they had to survive. Melandre rubbed her shoulder remembering the impact from the deathtalon.

The entrance was empty of people or creatures. The colorful trinket booths looked eerie under the emergency lights. She stopped and realized something had changed.

"Listen."

They all held perfectly still and tilted their heads.

"The sand storm has lessened," Natalya said.

Raul sighed in relief. "Rescue crews will be here in an hour tops."

A crouching shape to their right caught Melandre's eye. Natalya was looking straight at it as it slipped away down a tunnel.

"What was it?" she asked.

"I swear it was a lightning lizard," she said with her jaw hanging down.

Raul shook his head. "You're mistaken. We only had hywakaliths here. No hywlarkana."

"No, I'm certain," she said. "Dad showed me all of his notes. I saw the descriptions given by the locals. They have a hump in their back for the lightning organs. The hywakaliths kill with their teeth and don't have it."

"Must have been a shadow, or his notes were wrong," said Raul. "You've done quite well to this point with my expert help, but don't forget, you're still a little girl."

A stray thought tickled Melandre's memory. "Didn't you say a dome had been damaged two years ago while a week long sand storm raged?"

"Three days, but yeah."

"What dome was it?"

She knew the answer before he said the words. His eyes had gone wide as he realized the implications.

The lie was evident as soon as it left his lips. "It was the hyenas' dome."

She recalled that he mentioned before that the vegetation

had withstood the punishing winds and only a jungle could do that.

"Okay," she said. "I guess I'm wrong."

But they both knew the truth and that each other knew it. Even Natalya, who was sensitive to people's moods could tell something had happened.

As they crossed the courtyard, carefully watching all around them, Raul pointed to a tunnel on the right. "That one leads to the power center. What ever happened, happened there. Thankfully we don't need to bother with that."

Melandre stopped. She'd forgotten about their original plan once they'd gotten the shock codes and the revelation about the lizards.

"We should go there and see if we can turn the power back on. There might be other survivors," she said.

"Doubtful. You saw the carnage on the way here. I wouldn't be surprised if we were the only ones," Raul said.

Tears welled up in Natalya's eyes. "There were hundreds of people visiting the zoo."

Even though she herself had thought the same thing Raul had, when she looked at her daughter she knew they had to try. "There may be some, holed up in a safe spot. A lot of the predators have turned on each other."

"You can go if you want. I'm getting out to my vehicle," Raul said with his lips stretched across his yellow teeth. She knew he had other reasons to want to get out now. She just wished she could get her hands on Philippe's research again.

She checked with her kids to see what they wanted to do.

"The power station, mum." Natalya said while Andrake nodded his agreement.

"Good luck," Raul said as he headed toward the exit.

"Come with us," said Melandre. "We could use the help and there might be others we can save. It's the Institute's zoo after all."

"No way. I did my part helping you all get out. My vehicle is right outside this entrance not one hundred feet away." He pointed to the parking lot. "I'm taking my out while I'm alive. You'd be smart to do the same."

"We're the ones that helped you get out, you big dolt," Natalya said.

"Whatever you say," he said. "You'd better hurry if you want to be heroes before the authorities get here."

"You're the authority here," Melandre said, but Raul had already started limping away.

The three of them crept toward the tunnel that led to the power station and Melandre wondered if she was being an idiot risking her children's lives. She thought about all they'd done to get here and decided that they could do a little bit more. They had the wand.

The power station dome was a series of hallway. About half the emergency lights didn't work which Melandre thought strange. After peering into a few rooms and finding nothing but offices, they paused at a stairway going down.

"What was the bit between you and Mr. Hisler, mum? It looked like something awful had passed between you two," Natalya said in the dim light.

"It wasn't the hyenas' dome that broke and let the sand storm in for a few days. It'd been the hywakaliths'," she said. "Were there any births from the flower-toothed lizards?"

"Yeah," said Natalya. "About two years ago—" and then "—oh."

"What?" Andrake asked.

"The lightning lizard caused the power shutdown. They must have gotten old enough to create electricity and fried their computers. Unlucky for everyone involved that they took down the power center," Melandre said. "It's a shame we don't have Philippe's research. The lightning lizard proves your father's research is correct and they're sure to bury it now since their negligence has caused mass deaths."

Andrake looked to the floor.

"What, scamp?" she asked.

"Would you be mad if I told you I stole dad's data when you were transferring it to Mr. Hisler?" Andrake's shoulders were hunched.

Melandre grabbed her son and hugged him tight. "Oh my, no! That's the best thing you could have ever done. With a copy we can prove that your father was right!"

She felt like dancing, but they were still in a dangerous place. Melandre hesitated. "Maybe we should go back. This place looks deserted and I'm not sure what we'd do anyway. What do you two think?"

About that time, she noticed a low-slung shape ambling into the hallway between them and the entrance. Melandre tapped Andrake on his shoulder and pointed down the hall. "Quick, use your wand," she whispered.

But when he pointed it, nothing happened and the beastie started to move toward them.

"Down! Down!" she yelled as she saw the electricity gather in the creature's mouth.

They made it down the first flight when the ball of lightning roared over their heads and burst against the wall.

They hit the door at the bottom and pushed through it to see another set of stairs leading to another tunnel. They were in underground tunnels beneath the domes. The emergency lighting reflected across floor. Melandre couldn't figure it out until she hit the floor and it splashed.

The tunnels had been flooded by a few inches of water. They wouldn't be able to travel silently now. They ran down the tunnel, the water splashing loudly. She hoped there was only one lightning lizard. They followed the twists and turns, once taking a branch to the left, hoping the creature wasn't following until she stopped to listen and heard it splashing through the water behind them.

When they came into a wide room filled with pipes and power generation cylinders set in the water, she knew then why the power had gone out. They ran to the back wall, hoping to find an exit in the gloom, but no escape revealed itself. They were trapped.

The lightning lizard sauntered into the room as if it knew they had no escape. Its low body dragged a long scaly tail through the water. Melandre gripped the trash can lid and pushed her children behind her. She cast about for a platform or something to climb. Even if it didn't hit them with a direct lightning blast, the passive electricity would get them since they were standing ankle deep in the water.

The creature must have sensed her thoughts because it opened its mouth. Melandre was mesmerized by the gathering flickers in the beast's mouth as they danced from tooth to tooth. She knew they would die here unless she acted, but she didn't know what to do.

The electricity had gathered enough crackling mass and she knew it would release it soon. It didn't even have to hit them directly to kill.

Then she remembered the rubber boots they'd put on at the cthulhu-beast's dome. The boots would insulate them from the electricity.

Melandre shoved her children backwards in case her next move didn't work. She could at least die to save them.

"Get back and don't touch the water!"

As the lightning lizard released the ball, she launched the trashcan lid. The metal saucer flew through the air and impacted the lightning midway. The electricity expanded from the collision into the water. Melandre thought they were going to die when a blue haze washed across the water filling the surface in the room, making the lights flicker momentarily.

Instead they were left with a sickening burnt smell. Both she and her children were unharmed.

Across from them at the entrance, an immobile figure lay in the water. The lightning lizard had fried itself.

"We've got a new piece to add to Dad's research," said

Natalya. "The lightning lizards could probably make lightning in the jungles in the north, its just they would kill themselves if they were standing in water."

Melandre hugged her daughter. "Yeah. We can do that now, can't we?"

Andrake stared into the water. "Actually no," he said. "When mum pushed us back, I dropped the wand. The electricity fried it."

They all stared at it for a while until Melandre roused them. "Don't worry about it. The most important thing is that we're all still alive," she said. "Now let's get out of here, since we don't have the wand anymore and I don't think we can get the power back on with all this water."

They weaved back through the water soaked tunnels and up through the power center dome until they made their way to the exit, moving cautiously since they were without Andrake's hacking wand. Natalya had brought the lid at least.

As they crept along the trinket booths, they heard sirens in the distance. They ran out into the parking lot holding their hands to their face to block the gusting winds. The sand storm had abated, but the air was still blustery.

They had parked on the far side of the lot and she didn't want to risk going out that far so they stayed at the entrance, keeping a wary eye. As the line of flashing lights neared the zoo, Melandre pulled her children in tight.

Suddenly, she heard a commotion and her heart sunk.

Then she saw him. Raul was hopping on one leg and waving his crutch at the rescue vehicles. She was about to yell for him to be quiet when she saw the tempest.

The slick black creature that was built like a blade, unfolded its wings and timed a wind gust perfectly. About the time that Raul noticed the creature sailing toward him, he turned to run. The tempest blew past him and using its tail, speared him in the gut.

Melandre turned her children's faces away and had them hold their hands over their ears to block the screaming. The tempest closed its wings after it dragged Raul across the black pavement.

The rescue vehicles arrived in time to shoot the tempest, but Raul was already dead. They collected Melandre and her children and asked about survivors. She told them all she could, warning them about the myriad of beasts within and letting them know about the important information on Raul's corpse.

"Load the explosive rounds and get ready for close combat," said the commander to his assembled team. The hard clacks of clips slamming into place and shock-bayonets humming up to full charge filled the air.

The squad, in full battle armor, ran into the zoo as Melandre and her children were loaded into the back of a van. A pair of doctors started treating them. Melandre had them check her kids first as the van left the zoo.

With tears in her eyes, Melandre decided that when she got back to Steelzine, she would go straight to the authorities to make sure they didn't miss the evidence that would prove the Institute's role in the disaster. The Institute wouldn't be able to hide Philippe's research now.

And while she missed her husband dearly, she decided the worries she'd brought with her to the zoo were unfounded. She need not worry about raising their children alone. And while it would take them a little while to get over the shock of the events, they would be okay in the long run.

She let her gaze rest upon Natalya and Andrake, and smiled. They smiled back, relieved and sad all at the same time, and somehow without saying a thing, all their hands met in the middle in one tangled heap and they looked out the back of the van.

The sand storm had blown the green corrosion from the domes until they were a polished copper shine. With the sunlight slipping through the remnants of the storm, the domes were beautiful reddish-brown jewels scattered against the gap in the hills. But as they rumbled back to Steelzine, the sun slipped behind a cloud, dousing the zoo in shadow. And Melandre could only think that the domes - with the ochre dust pooled around them - looked like bloody stones dropped by a careless child.

More Real Than Flesh

written by

Grayson Bray Morris

ABOUT THE AUTHOR
Grayson Bray Morris grew up shy and awkward in North Carolina, a good student but a lousy socializer. Along the way she picked up social skills and studied mathematics, then computer graphics. She worked for a while at IBM as an assembly-language programmer, then went on to BOPS, a spinoff, and had a marvelous time programming on a parallel DSP. After two failed marriages (producing one daughter) she met and married a Dutchman, had three more babies, and moved to the Netherlands. Her passion for languages led her to translation. She's written all her life, but only recently for an audience. Visit her on the web at www.graysonbraymorris.com.

More Real Than Flesh

The day's first customer walked through Petch's door. He was slender, not ugly, reasonably clean-cut: better than she was used to. But the glint in his eyes was pure sadist. He would want pain, and blood, and probably death.

They all wanted those things. What was it in this one that frightened her?

The john was already sitting down across from her. Petch smiled at him, a little lopsided to highlight that she was flesh. Up close, the johns could see the lines creasing the corners of her eyes; her tight dresslet played up the imperfection of her tits. Karson had cupped his hands around those tits the day she showed up looking for work, fifteen and lost and really, really hungry, and said, "Left one's half again bigger than the right. Sweet Jesus, they'll pay double for you."

The john let his unaugmented gaze travel from her eyes down to her exposed crotch, like they all did. When she figured he was halfway through gaping, Petch fidgeted a little; fidgeting was so hard for a sexbot to get right. The john watched her fingers move on the arm of the chair, watched her left knee bump into her right as she shifted her weight. She was the real deal.

He looked back up into her eyes, lingering a fraction of a second on her mouth, and Petch realized what scared her about him: he knew how to kill her. Really kill her, for good.

Petch gave herself ten seconds to feel the weight of her life pressing down. Why couldn't she have a sweet one, just once? There were plenty of decent johns looking for connection in a world where touch was a second-class sense, hungry to fumble through awkward sex instead of getting digital feedback-loop ecstasy with somebody's perfect avatar. A john who wanted to walk in, short and fat with mousy brown hair or tall and skinny and balding, and have a short, fat mousy girl with uneven tits take him by the hand and fuck him. Really fuck him, not just send a packet of bits over the net and stimulate his neural feed.

But Karson didn't traffic in those johns. He catered to the ones who wanted to slice thin lines into a girl's skin, to squeeze her throat and feel it spasm beneath their hands. Who wanted to punish her for being born to imperfect flesh. Petch had perfected the art of dropping herself at just the right time, slumping into lifelessness so naturally no john had ever suspected he didn't kill her himself. And, conveniently, notifying tech that end game had been reached so they could get her out of there in time.

But this one knew. And he'd gotten past Karson.

Petch smiled at the john as she slid her lower jaw forward. His eyes widened and he lunged for her, but she bit down hard, sliding her right upper canine into the lower first molar and making contact. She felt his hands grab her mouth, but he was too late. She was gone, and Karson's boys would be there in seconds, before he had time to cut her up while her blood was still warm.

§

Out in the real world, Petch was beautiful. Her avatar was tall and thin, with an hourglass waist and perfect tits. As soon as she left the shielding in Karson's compound, the net read out her stream, her optical feed kicked in, and she was a normal girl in the normal world.

Not that Karson let her out much. Two or three times a week, he'd let a couple of the girls go into town with some of his tech boys. Chaperones, Karson said, to make sure nobody gave his girls any trouble.

They made it damned hard to find the keymaker.

Petch hadn't always known about the keymaker. The first time she bolted, climbing out the bathroom window at a club, she woke up disoriented, staring at Karson's amused face. She hadn't known he could drop her from a distance; she thought maybe she'd fainted, and the tech boy had brought her back in. "Little girl, you can't ever get away from me," Karson had grinned at her. "I hold the keys to your soul." She'd thought he was being poetic.

But the third time, when the whole damned misery of being so thoroughly owned kept her from opening her eyes right away after they'd shunted her back to life, she heard Karson say, "Tell the keymaker to reconfigure her lockdown to twenty yards. She damn near made it into the street, and the wetware ain't worth jack if she gets her body run over."

She'd thought he meant the expensive, illegal, military-grade backup chips he'd put in her head would be damaged, and he'd lose her. Later, she realized the soul whose keys he held was worthless to him, just necessary software pulling the strings of her lucrative flesh.

§

Karson let her take one of the tech boys into town to watch the latest immersive vid. Beforehand, drinking lattes in the square as they watched a particularly talented morph artist run through his show, the tech boy said, "Keymaker's not far from here."

Petch nearly dropped her coffee. She pulled the tech boy's feed into focus, but he was still watching the morph artist like he hadn't spoken.

It was a test. If Karson found out she knew about the keymaker again, he'd wipe her, and she'd have to start all over. Motherfucker never wiped any of her working memories; he left every miserable death bright in her mind, taking only the little things that made her life bearable. Like knowing there was a keymaker.

The worst part always came right after she found out again, after the bright searing hope sliced up through her and made tears sting her eyes. When the knowledge tapped inactive wetbits into resonance, like deja vu, and she realized she'd known this before, and before again, going back for years, and every time, Karson had taken it from her.

"I'm sorry, what?"

"I'll take you to him."

Not very subtle, Karson. You got to pick them better than that if you want me to fall for it. "Who? Some new john? Karson tell you to make me work before the show?" It didn't matter, Petch realized. Karson was going to wipe her whether she feigned innocence or not. "Ah, shit," she said, throwing her latte to the ground. The rolling cup briefly intruded on the feeds of several nearby patrons before the café software filtered it out of its stream.

"This is the day you've been waiting for, Petch." The tech boy's avatar still watched the show with smiling interest, but he'd unlocked his stream for her. She switched him to camera input and looked at the thin, pockmarked young man across the table. He wasn't bored, wasn't fidgeting, none of the usual tells. He was just watching her eyes.

Petch stared at him silently. "Why do you care?" she said at last.

The tech boy smiled at her before he looked away. "Because you pay me to."

§

The next ten minutes were a series of wetbit cascades, the tech boy accessing her forgotten memories until Petch thought she'd go mad.

"Karson pays for the Class II wetware, then skimps on the wipes," the tech boy said. "He should pay for full erase capability instead of just unlinking the memories in the personal module." He leaned forward. "Look, Petch, I've caught you up to speed, and now we've got to get moving if we're going to be done before Karson decides we've been gone too long and drops you."

"Will he drop you, too?" Petch asked.

The tech boy shook his head. "Karson buys tech loyalty the old-fashioned way, with free snatch and plenty of bling. No extra chips in our heads." He tapped behind one ear. "No restart if we disappoint him, either. So let's get going, okay?"

Petch stopped cold. "I can't be paying you enough to take that kind of gamble."

He just smiled at her.

"You've been helping me for a long time," she said, realizing.

He nodded.

"I don't remember you. Not much." She had only sketchy memories of the tech boy, coming in to revive her after a john had gone, behind a desk in Karson's office when she came in for a bitcheck.

He shrugged and looked away. "Sometimes bits get lost."

Sometimes bits get lost. Friendship gets lost, just like that. Petch had custom wetware in her head that nobody had access to, top of the line state of the art sexbot-and-soldier fucking wetware, and sometimes bits got lost.

"Do I forget you every time he wipes me?" she asked.

He shook his head, still looking out across the square. "Just this time. Just a shitty fluke of the bits."

But he hadn't seemed surprised. Hadn't asked her if she remembered him now, after the cascade.

It was hard to believe every single personal memory she had of him was lost. Maybe she hadn't had any. Maybe he was just a puppy in love from afar, a soft heart crying over a broken, damaged flesh whore.

He was still open to her, still in the flesh, but she'd kept her stream locked to him. She had to; she needed every second she could get out here, in public, where privacy law meant people only saw her in the flesh if *she* let them. But memories or no, he was risking his life for her.

"Kirit," she said. The least she could do was call him by name. He turned back to her, a question on his face, and maybe a little hope.

Petch took a deep breath and made her avatar reflect the embarrassment she felt. "I'm sorry, I can't unlock my stream for you." She looked straight into his eyes. They were bright blue, so vivid it was amazing they were his flesh eyes; for a moment they made him beautiful, and almost familiar.

Kirit nodded. He stared at her with his vivid, too-large eyes, and she watched them trace a line down her face, over her shoulder, as if he were brushing back a lock of her hair. Her flesh hair, long because Karson said it had to be. She kept it short in the real world.

"I see what's underneath every day, Petch," he finally said. "I also see what's inside." He tapped his head. "Karson's never even bothered to look." He relocked his stream, and his blond, gym-rat avatar replaced the skinny boy in Petch's feed. "That's why he'll never know you're gone."

Petch's heart raced. "Today is different," she said.

He nodded. "Today we switch you out."

§

Petch's hidden account, to which she'd apparently been siphoning credits in invisible tens and twenties from her pay and from the shopping money Karson gave her for her trips to town, had reached eighty thousand last night. Sixteen years of saving, at first just because it made her feel she had some kind of control, later because she was planning her escape.

Petch didn't remember being so close to goal, even after Kirit told her. He just shrugged and looked away. "Sometimes bits get lost," he said again.

She had enough to buy a Class II sexbot, the kind sold as wives to rich old men, with modules that made conversation and emulated feelings, with bodies that were hard to tell from flesh; and, after that, she still had enough to pay the keymaker.

Kirit transferred payment to the café bill feed and bought two vid tickets they wouldn't use. Two minutes after they left the café square, he turned into an alley that didn't exist.

Somebody had a lot of savvy, locking out the public camera stream like that. No seams where the generated bricks met the ordinary ones, no feed hiccups between the streams.

Kirit's leg stuck back through the hacked-in wall, into the range of the cameras. The leg in Petch's feed was pale above scuffed sneakers; Kirit had turned his stream completely off. He leaned forward and stuck his face through. "Petch," he said softly. "I know it's hard, but you're going to have to turn off your stream here."

Petch balked, and he smiled at her. "It's okay. I still know who you really are."

"But they don't," she said, gesturing. "I want them to see the real me, only the real me, not that."

"Petch, the keymaker has to drop you anyway to make the switch. And the rest aren't going to see you at all. All they'll see is a big, fat stream of credits coming in, and believe me, they'll think you're beautiful."

She hesitated ten seconds, then twenty, until the fear took hold, that Karson might drop her and wipe her and make her wait another month, another year. Another second.

That he might drop Kirit for good, really kill him, because of her.

He had been a friend to her, the pockmarked boy with the bright blue eyes. But that wasn't really him; the real Kirit, the one he'd created, was smooth, blond, tanned and muscled. Now that she'd seen his avatar, it was rude of her to think of him as anything else, as the accidental flesh he'd been born into.

Yet she was glad he'd kept his avatar eyes the same, beautiful blue.

Petch switched off her stream and took Kirit's outstretched hand.

§

"You'll miss it at first," the keymaker told her. "Your old body. But soon enough you'll get used to the new one."

Petch watched the sexbot wetware in her old body wake up on the platform beside her, watched the keymaker check its vitals. Her old body looked around the room, taking in Petch, the keymaker, Kirit.

Kirit was watching Petch.

"I've got to take her back," he said. "Before Karson drops her."

Petch's new belly soared like a roller coaster. No one would ever drop her again. Kirit smiled at her, but his eyes were somber.

"Does she think she's me?" Petch asked. "Will she pass?" What she meant was, *are you going to survive this?*

"I copied in your memories of the work, your name, your personal details," the keymaker said. "As long as no one questions her too closely, she'll pass."

"Can she fidget?" Petch asked. If the johns complained, Kirit would die.

The short, fat sexbot with uneven tits bumped her knees together in answer, tapping her fingers on the platform padding, wiggling her toes, smiling Petch's lopsided smile.

"Karson will never suspect," Kirit said. "But I'll miss you."

"I'll miss you, too," Petch said. And though it felt like she'd only met him today, she knew she would. But the keymaker was wrong; she wouldn't miss her old body at all. It had never been real; *this* body, now, this body was real. Tall, thin, with an hourglass waist and perfect tits.

But Kirit just kept staring at her eyes.

The Watcher

written by

George Walker

ABOUT THE AUTHOR
George Walker is an engineer working for a high tech company in Portland, Oregon, USA. His fiction has appeared in Ideomancer, Science Fiction Age, Tomorrow SF, Steampunk Tales, Reflection's Edge, Helix SF, Electric Spec, Spectra Magazine *and elsewhere. Some of his fiction can be found at http://sites.google.com/site/georgeswalker/.*

The Watcher

It wasn't a whale. The sound approaching the sub beneath the Indian Ocean was no living thing.

Inside the DisneySub, Shabana was piloting in Virtual, her senses disconnected from her body. Initially, she thought the beating noise came from a surface ship, filtered through the thermal layer above. She'd slowed the *Lotus* to look for whales, and its fluidic drive was barely active. Six hundred feet under the surface, below the reach of sunlight or radio signals, she floated through water dark as ink.

"Only five more minutes, Shabana," said Captain Singh. "We've a schedule to keep." His avatar, a lanternfish, glowed with bioluminescence in the darkness beside her.

The DisneySub was on its daily cruise from India to Sri Lanka. Captain Singh and Shabana were part of a crew of four: three Indians and one American. They were responsible for two hundred paying passengers. On some trips, a probe would find a pod of whales to show to tourists on the holographic interior walls. Today, only fish and squid.

And something else.

"UV-1's reached the thermal layer," announced Patel, controlling a probe via ghostwire. His avatar was with the probe. "The rumble you hear is a submarine reactor. I estimate it's less than a mile away."

"Indian Navy?" asked the captain.

"Here in the Gulf of Mannar?" said Patel. "It had *better* be ours."

"Keep *Lotus* here a little longer, Shabana," said the captain. "If we can't find the passengers a whale, a Navy sub will do."

"It's not trying to hide," said Patel. "Their sonar pinged me, but I doubt they noticed the tiny reflection. I used their sonar to find them: 2800 feet from UV-1."

"Get closer," said the captain. "Spin as much cable as you need." The DisneySub had sixteen spinnerets to manufacture nanotube ghostwire for the probes. Almost unbreakable when first spun, it would dissolve within a day.

"No need," said Patel. "It's heading straight at me."

That made Shabana uneasy. *Lotus* was on a charted course. "Why would the Navy stalk us?"

The lanternfish vanished. The captain must have joined Patel at UV-1. Shabana was pilot; her duty was to stay with *Lotus*. She kept most of her Virtual presence in the ocean, but let her hearing pass ghost-like through the passenger decks. Conversation buzzed, along with the occasional sing-song quack of an animatronic duck delivering food or drink. Yesterday,

Lotus had hosted an English wedding party. Today nearly all the passengers were Indian: company men showing clients their off-shore operations, families on vacation, a group of Indian imperialists en route to a rally, some Buddhists traveling to a retreat.

The lanternfish appeared beside her.

"The sub found our probe," said the captain. "Patel's turned on coherent lamps to get holography for Norman to display on the walls." Norman was their white-haired DisneyCorp media advisor.

"Is it–?" she began. But the fish vanished, and Shabana was in the dark again.

A minute later, in addition to the steady rumble, she heard a high-pitched whine. Then the shock of a pressure wave struck her.

The lanternfish was back. "Emergency dive! Now!"

Shabana sucked in ballast, feeding full power from the fuel cells to the fluidic drive. *Lotus* darted squid-like toward the bottom of the sea.

"What happened?" She swam in the dark, fast as she could.

"It's a Pakistani sub!"

After a moment, the lanternfish vanished, replaced by Patel's avatar, a deep-sea anglerfish.

"You threw the passengers to the floor," he complained.

"What happened to the probe?"

"A torpedo destroyed it. Keep diving! I'll release another probe in our wake." The anglerfish vanished.

India and Pakistan weren't at war, but engaged in endless

border incidents. Shabana hadn't thought of the Indian Ocean as their border until now.

She felt sonar pinging her skin. She was nearly a thousand feet below the surface, and the DisneySub, with its commercial carbon fiber hull, couldn't go much deeper. A titanium-hulled military sub could dive thousands of feet deeper. In Virtual, the pressure bio-feedback was making it hard for her to breathe, as if her ribs were bending in sympathy with the hull struts.

The lanternfish was back. "Turn to starboard," said the captain. "Take us into Kodai Canyon." His avatar looked almost two-dimensional, as if crushed by the depth.

Shabana spun on *Lotus*'s axis like a paramecium and swam into the canyon. "It's still tracking us," she warned.

"Doesn't matter. A propeller-driven sub's not maneuverable enough to follow us here. Level out."

"Do the passengers know what's going on?"

"Yes. Norman showed them holography from UV-1."

"Did I hurt anyone?"

"What matter? You saved them. But their anger has turned both passenger decks into cobra nests. I retreated our animatronics to protect them from damage."

The sonar striking *Lotus*'s hull was indirect now, reflecting off canyon walls. The Pakistani sub knew they were here, but couldn't see them to launch a torpedo.

"Slow to stop and jack out," said Singh.

Shabana felt uneasy leaving the sub unguarded, but did as ordered. She emerged from Virtual into *Lotus*'s control center, squinting even though the light was dim. Her white Disney uniform was a blaze of light in comparison with the depths. The bearded Captain Singh, wearing his Sikh turban, was strapped in the control chair to her left, and Patel was to her right. Norman stood. Too old for implants, he couldn't enter Virtual.

"Are you getting more holography?" asked the captain.

Patel nodded. "It's definitely Pakistani."

"They must have seen our passenger manifest: The group of Indian imperialists. Kumar is leading them personally."

"Why are they taking a cruise?" asked Norman. "Why didn't they just fly?"

"Kumar's on the no-fly list," said Singh.

"That sub can stay submerged forever," said Shabana, twisting long black hair around her fingers, "but we have less than eight hours left."

"And no way to call for help down here," said the captain. "We need a plan. Ideas?"

"In the movie *Travels with Sacagawea*," said the old man, "there's a scene where she negotiates for safe passage through–"

"What? You don't negotiate with Pakistanis!" Patel's voice dripped scorn.

"Maybe that's what they say about Indian imperialists," said Norman.

"This is America's fault for selling submarines to Pakistan," said Patel. He stared at the old man coldly.

"That's not new. In the film *Davy Crockett: Warpath!* the U.S. Calvary sells rifles to both tribes."

"Are we just a tribe to you?!"

"It worked in the film," Norman muttered.

"It's time to stop asking what Snow White would do," said Singh. "You're from DisneyCorp. What do you know about *Lotus* that might help us?"

"All he knows is movies," grumbled Patel.

Shabana felt blind sitting here. "Someone has to keep watch," she said. "Tell me what you decide." She jacked in.

She was back in the dark water, feeling its pressure. The sonar from the Pakistani sub behind her provided a ghost image of the canyon, and she overlaid that image with the underwater map. None of the channels led to Sri Lanka. *Lotus* might buy time, but not escape. She felt fragile and defenseless. The sensation of crushed ribs reinforced that. A predator lurked above, waiting to snap her neck.

After a few minutes, the lanternfish joined her.

"What's the decision?" she asked.

"We'll try waiting them out," said the captain. "Every hour we're late to Sri Lanka, the more worried the authorities. They'll send hover-drones, then submersibles. That should drive off the Pakistani sub."

"And our passengers..."

"–have no say. I am captain."

It wasn't much of a plan. She decided to take a closer look at the other sub.

The black leviathan was suspended above Patel's probe, and he'd left the imaging lamps on. The sub wasn't moving, but sounded like a thing alive – its nuclear heart beating as it watched and waited. The probe was close enough for her to almost touch individual rivets in the hologram. The giant blades at the sub's tail were frozen in mid-turn, reflecting the lamps. Turning her viewpoint, she couldn't see *Lotus* from the probe; it was too far away, below and ahead of the sub.

"Do they know we're watching them?" Shabana called to Singh.

"Undoubtedly. They've given us distance, daring us to run."

"Did our DisneyCorp advisor have any advice?"

"He listed our assets. We have *Lotus* and a few UVs left and all the animatronics. Plus the four of us. Why does DisneyCorp send along an advisor who knows nothing useful?"

At the probe, Shabana heard a dull clang and a gurgle of water from the other sub. "What was that?"

Then she heard a high-pitched whine, and rapid pings against the probe, then *Lotus*'s skin. She felt a sense of panic.

"Torpedo!" said Singh.

Shabana urged *Lotus* forward. Even with fluidic drive, it took seconds for her to gather speed from a dead stop. She jettisoned Patel's probe.

"I didn't think they could see us!"

"Find a refuge," said Singh. "That upper side channel!" He neon-flashed it for her in the map-view.

The ping spacing dopplered up against Shabana's skin as the torpedo closed in on *Lotus*.

"I'll be trapped there!"

"We can't outrun a torpedo. But it can't turn like we can. Take it as tight as you can."

Shabana waited until she was almost to the channel, then

banked *Lotus* sideways ninety degrees, flat belly forward. She felt painful pressure feedback, hearing her outer hull groan as it flexed. *Lotus* slowed dramatically, but she still overshot the channel, narrowly missing an underwater cliff.

Shabana reversed at full power, swimming backward into the channel above the main trench.

The torpedo shot past her, slamming into the cliff she'd barely avoided, and exploded. The shock wave struck her like a hammer blow. Rocks showered *Lotus*'s hull, scouring swaths of biomimetic cilia from it.

Shabana was deaf and blind in the ocean. Silt and echoes smothered her.

"Down! Down!" said Singh. "Become as Death!"

She killed her floodlights and sucked in ballast, sinking to the floor of the side channel. Her bottom crunched onto sand and rocks, and silt settled on top of her. She froze the fluidic drive. Pings from the Pakistani sub were muffled and distorted now. It had lost her.

"Jack out," ordered the captain.

Shabana emerged shakily from Virtual into *Lotus*'s control center. Norman was sitting on the floor. He held a red-stained handkerchief to his forehead.

"There are many passenger injuries," said Patel. "Were you trying to turn upside down?"

"I..."

"Quiet!" snapped Singh. "We're alive, aren't we?"

"Yes," grumbled Norman. "Thanks for asking."

"Maybe they won't find us," said Shabana in a hoarse

whisper.

"They'll detect there was no implosion," said Patel, "no floating debris. They won't leave without finishing us off."

"Someone should meet with the passengers," said Norman.

"Is that what is says in your corporate manual?" asked Patel. "Put on a costume and lead them in song?"

"They're human beings," said Norman.

"We don't have time," snapped the captain.

"Maybe we should send the animatronics back in," said Shabana.

"Let me change the media on the walls," said Norman. "The *20,000 Leagues Under the Sea* visuals are the last thing they want to see now." He paused. "Perhaps *Jungle Book*?"

An alarm sounded.

Patel jacked in briefly, then re-opened his eyes. "Some passengers have breached a hatch to a service tunnel."

The captain cursed.

"Those aren't your typical passengers," said Norman.

"Kumar's men?" asked Singh.

Patel nodded. "They'll cause us as much trouble as the Pakistanis."

"Shabana, jack in and watch for the other sub. We'll stop the passengers somehow."

She nodded. "Protect my mortal shell."

"We'll guard the meat," said Patel. "You guard *Lotus*."

Shabana entered the ocean in Virtual. It was a different environment now. Not free-swimming in the open, but trapped like a crab in a hole. She tasted mud in the saltwater and shivered from the cold. High above her, she imagined sunshine, waves and seagulls. Here in the dark depths, tons of seawater pressed in on her from all sides. She looked at the map. In this channel, the sea floor rose gradually toward a broad shelf. An exposed, vulnerable shelf.

She didn't have a magic ticket home, a way to turn invisible. What she did have, though, was a way to simulate a thousand different escapes.

She tried every possible route: to Sri Lanka; back to India; hiding and waiting; surfacing and deploying rafts; even ramming the enemy sub.

She died a thousand times.

When it was over, she was back where she started, with no way out.

The lanternfish appeared beside her.

"Shabana! Jack out!"

She opened her eyes in the control center. Patel's control chair was empty. She looked around. Norman was gone, too.

"Where–"

"Kumar's men and his fellow passengers captured Patel," said Singh. "I'd sent him to barricade the hatches."

"Do Kumar's men know where we are?"

"Not yet. And Patel is a man of honor. He won't talk. I don't trust the American, though. You have to find him."

"Where?"

"Just find him!"

Shabana jumped into *Lotus* in Virtual: On the lower passenger deck, some of the passengers were bleeding, but the

Buddhists had calmed them. Some passengers were meditating. A little girl sat on her worried mother's lap, clutching a stuffed Minnie Mouse and watching the walls, where monkeys swung through the trees of Kipling's *Jungle Book*.

Shabana jumped to the upper deck. It was half-empty, and she saw the breached hatch leading to the service tunnels. She jumped through it into a tunnel lit only by LEDs, and heard the hiss of recyclers extracting carbon dioxide from the air.

She found men in the narrow tunnels, but couldn't tell how many were Kumar's men and how many were passengers he'd recruited. They'd spread through the tunnels like ants, looking for the crew.

It took time to find Norman. He wasn't in the crew's break room or anywhere near the control room. She found him in the very forward section of *Lotus*, in the probe launch compartment. Music from the previous century blasted from the speakers: "Yellow Submarine" by the Beatles.

The old man was kneeling on the floor, surrounded by animatronics. A faded, empty Disney Princesses backpack lay on the floor. It must have been Norman's. She saw an open toolkit and a pile of game control wands nearby. The old man was attaching a ghostwire connector to a duckling.

She remotely switched off his music.

Norman looked up, startled. "Who's there?"

"Shabana," she said through a speaker.

"Oh." He looked relieved.

With his music turned off, she now heard muffled singing: a tinny chorus of "It's a Small World." Norman had duct-taped shut the mouths and bills of the animatronics.

"What are you doing?" she asked.

He looked around at the animatronics and his tools. "Just sending the seven dwarves out to do a little mining."

"They're not dwarves, and you have more than seven."

"I'm prepared for attrition."

"The captain says you need to come back," she said.

He glanced behind him. "Unfortunately, I had a little trouble with the door."

She looked at the blackened hatch. It was welded shut from the inside.

Norman said, "Has the captain given you his *We're all soldiers now* speech?"

"No."

"He will."

"What *are* you doing?"

"Do you remember the fishing trawler scene in *The Little Mermaid and the Lost Treasure of Atlantis*?"

"No," she said irritably. "Was it 2-D?"

"All the classics were 2-D. Anyway, it doesn't matter. You'd probably think I was nuts."

I already know that, Norman.

He resumed work on the connector, then released the duckling. "What does Singh expect me to do? Before, he said I should go sleep in a film vault. 'Disneyworld isn't a real world,' he said."

"If all of us stay together..."

"We can perish together? He has no plan." Norman

grabbed another animatronic and began unscrewing its service panel.

"We have to do something!" said Shabana.

"I *am* doing something. And I could use a hand here. But you're just a ghost, aren't you?"

"Soon, we'll all be ghosts."

"What will you come back as, Shabana?"

"Say again?"

"Don't you people reincarnate?" he asked.

"Is that something you saw in a movie?"

"Everything I know, I learned from watching movies."

"You're pathetic, Norman!"

He shrugged. "I might call you later."

"And I might not answer," Shabana snapped. She jacked out.

In the control center, she told the captain, "I found him."

"Good! Is he on his way?"

"No. He's playing with his toys."

"That American...*lunatic!*"

"At least he's locked in where can't betray us."

Singh stroked his beard, nostrils flaring. "I should never have let Patel go. He's the security officer, but that was beyond his responsibility. Everything is my responsibility. The captain goes down with the ship."

"We sink every day," she reminded him.

He glared at her. "Is this is a joke to you? We're at war now. Pakistan has made everyone on board a soldier."

"I only meant–"

He stood up. "I have to talk to Kumar about the Pakistanis."

"He'll take you hostage, just like Patel!"

"I'm the captain."

"That makes no sense! And what about me?"

"Your honor is not at stake. Stay here. Set the security bolts for the hatch after I leave."

"Before, you said we should stay together!"

"That was before I realized I was a soldier."

After he left, Shabana set the bolts. No one to watch over her now. She was afraid to jack in, because it would leave her defenseless: The control room was the only place on board with no cameras for Virtual. And if Singh changed his mind, she wouldn't hear him pounding on the hatch.

"We're all going to die," she whispered.

There was an old fashioned monitor, the one Norman used to change the wall media. Compared to Virtual, it was like trying to perform surgery using her feet. She switched awkwardly from camera to camera inside the sub. She caught glimpses of men in the tunnels, but when they moved, it was too hard to follow. She couldn't find either Patel or Singh. She watched the passengers on the lower deck for a little while. No rioting or smashed hatches. Children were watching the jungle on the walls. Their parents were the anxious ones.

Frustrated by the primitive interface, she returned to her seat and jacked in, returning to her sandy tomb. The propeller noise from the Pakistani sub throbbed somewhere in the distance. She couldn't see anything, but felt the pressure of the deep. She wished she'd deployed a probe before setting down, because something new was out there; she sensed motion in the water close to *Lotus*. Then she remembered Norman talking about dwarves.

In Virtual, she jumped to the probe launch compartment. Norman had turned his music back on, but the ducklings, the mice, all the animatronics were gone. The old man stood in front of a wide shelf, staring at a holo-panel set in the wall and swinging his arms vigorously as if conducting *Fantasia*. He had a game wand in each hand, and there were more of them on the shelf. He was sweating and panting. Periodically, he set down one wand to quickly pick up another.

"Norman?" she said.

He continued as if he hadn't heard her.

"Where are the animatronics?" she asked. When he didn't answer, she linked to the holographic image he was watching.

A menagerie of animatronics moved in the ocean outside *Lotus*, floating upward. She could make out their little four-fingered hands in the holographic feed. Machines designed for serving drinks and waving to children made poor swimmers. Their movements were slow and jerky underwater.

Norman must have ejected them one by one via the probe launch tube. She counted sixteen, each linked via ghostwire to the sub's nanotube spinnerets. Instead of using Virtual avatars, each was tagged in his holographic feed with a hexadecimal index: 0 through 9, A through F. She realized that the animatronics were no longer controlled by the bar's computer, but by the old man's pile of primitive game wands.

"You turned on one of the outside lamps," she accused. "Don't you know we're hiding?"

He seemed to hear that. "It's just like *Finding Nemo*, Shabana," he panted. "The sharks, the hunt. And a few new additions." He switched wands again.

"Why?"

"I'll never get another chance to direct a scene like this."

"You think this is a movie?!"

Norman was sweating, switching wands, concentrating on the animatronics. "Our other options were limited."

"We die in all the options."

"This one depends on my performance." He panted, swallowing. "Shabana, I can save us. Trust me."

Worried about what might be happening in the control center, she jacked out.

Something was battering the control room hatch, and she saw the wall vibrate with each blow.

"Shabana!" It was Captain Singh shouting, and she could hear he wasn't alone.

"You led them here!" she accused.

"Shabana, I have talked to Kumar–"

"And you led him here!"

Shabana stayed in her control chair, fists clenched. Nothing would be gained by going to the hatch. She couldn't stop them by leaning against it. If the bolts didn't hold, nothing would.

"Shabana! Kumar has a plan. He and his men smuggled guns on board. The Pakistanis don't know that. If we surface, they will try to board to take Kumar, and we will fight them."

"The other sub won't let us surface. I've done the simulations. Where is Patel? Let me talk to him."

"He's unconscious. Kumar's men beat him when he wouldn't talk."

"Does that make him more honorable than you?"

"You know nothing of honor!"

The old-fashioned phone in the control center rang. She picked up. "Norman?"

"Come here! I need you!" He hung up.

"Was that Norman?" asked Singh.

"Yes. He has a plan." *One as foolhardy as yours.*

"Are you with us, or that lunatic? I order you to—"

She jacked in.

The sound of the Pakistani sub was dangerously close, chewing a path through the deep like an avatar of Shiva the Destroyer. Shabana felt its sonar on her skin and turned on lights and sonar. She spit out saltwater ballast, raising *Lotus* from the seabed, and fed power to her fluidic drive. Silt roiled in the water around her.

Through ghostwire, she sensed Norman's servants high above her in the ocean, spread out with cables between the animatronics like a giant spider web.

"Release the cables!" she called to him.

"I'm waiting for the other sub to reach the net!"

She swam out of the shallow channel, up above the sea shelf, exposed at last. There was no choice. She listened with dread for the sound of a torpedo tube flooding.

Behind her, the Pakistani sub reached the net and glided

between the animatronics, closing on her.

She felt Norman release cables from all the spinnerets.

Behind her, ghostwire snagged on the enemy sub's conning tower and control vanes. As the net collapsed in on itself, the sub effortlessly towed the lifeless menagerie behind it. Ducklings and mice spun in its wake, tightening the net around the sub. Thousands of feet of nanotube cable began wrapping around rudders and propeller. The blades chopped up animatronics, scattering fur and feathers in its wake, but the nearly unbreakable cables continued to tighten.

She heard a torpedo tube flooding.

Then the Pakistani sub veered to starboard as tangled ghostwire cables forced control vanes to new angles. Its propeller began slowing, then jammed. The sub drifted, continuing to turn away from *Lotus*, and she felt a thrill of hope.

"Too bad about the ducklings," said Norman. "It was my first time directing."

Shabana laughed. "You've watched too many movies." She rode *Lotus* close to the ocean floor, the gap between the two subs widening as she sped toward Sri Lanka.

Made in the USA
Charleston, SC
29 August 2011